MACADOO
of the Maury River

MACADOO

of the Maury River

* * *

GIGI AMATEAU

CANDLEWICK PRESS

Copyright © 2013 by Gigi Amateau
Frontispiece illustration copyright © 2013 by Lindsey Windfelt

First paperback edition 2015

Library of Congress Catalog Card Number 2013931459
ISBN 978-0-7636-3766-8 (hardcover)
ISBN 978-0-7636-7670-4 (paperback)

14 15 16 17 18 19 BVG 10 9 8 7 6 5 4 3 2 1

Printed in Berryville, VA, U.S.A.

This book was typeset in Horley Old Style.

Candlewick Press
99 Dover Street
Somerville, Massachusetts 02144

visit us at www.candlewick.com

For my sis

CONTENTS

Ask the animals, and they will teach you.
Ask the birds, and they will tell you.

Or speak with the earth, and it will teach you.
Even the fish will relate the story to you.

What creature doesn't know that the
Lord's hands made it?

The life of every living creature and the spirit
in every human body are in his hands.

Job 12:7

✴ CHAPTER ONE ✴

A Great Belgian

In his darkest hour, a friend once asked, "What if they sell me?"

Such fear tangled up in that question: *What if I am not needed, no longer useful? What if I am not wanted, no longer loved? What if I am forgotten?*

The quiver in his voice pierced my heart, plunged through flesh, blood, and bone and into memory. "What if they sell me?" he asked.

Here is how I answered.

I was born at a place for breeding horses but not for keeping them, in Alberta, far from the Maury River where I call home now.

I remember as a yearling I surveyed my pasture and the jagged gray mountains beyond the fence.

"If you dare, just try to beat me!" I called. I raced past every mare grazing in the summer grasses, and I dashed by every foal standing in the rocky field. The colts and the fillies gave chase, but I crested the hill first, many lengths ahead of them all.

When the fastest filly caught up, she head-butted me, slamming into my shoulder with all her strength, but it wasn't enough to move me. I stood on the tip of a great boulder jutting out from the ground, and, like the stone beneath me, I would not be moved — not by the wind and not by the filly.

I nickered for her to come at me again. "One more try," I urged her.

She spun around, pawed at the ground, and made a big show of snorting. She backed up and charged. This time, I dodged her battery, and the filly fell down into the tall grass.

"I'm king of the hill!" I proclaimed. "Bow down to serve me."

A cabbage butterfly of silken cream, unconcerned with my victory over the filly, lit across the white clover blossoms. She circled my cannon and flitted down my hoof. She fanned her wings, came softly to rest on the grass, and tickled my foot with her legs. Butterfly kisses.

The filly — a draft like me — was strong and power-ful. The butterfly looked delicate and fragile.

"I can play gently, butterfly. You're safe with me," I reassured her.

The butterfly darted around my ear and then dis-appeared away down the hill. Because I was enchanted with the butterfly, I didn't see or hear anything else happening until I heard the mares sounding an alarm.

Our caretaker, Janey, had left a new farmhand in charge for the day. He had let the stallion into the wrong field by mistake, then walked away. The stallion shouldn't have been let into our pasture. Mixing up stallions and colts wasn't a good idea and could endan-ger the mares and the weanlings.

When I heard the mares shouting, I forgot my butterfly game of wings and flight. I needed a place to hide. I turned to bolt, but before I or the filly could run, a long, dark shadow overtook us.

Behind me a voice bellowed, "Little horse, why don't *you* tell *me* who is king of the hill?"

Stepping out of my blind spot, a blond stallion appeared. A white blaze ran the length of his face, and white socks painted all four legs. His coat glistened. Every rippled muscle from his neck to his hocks pulsed as if it were its own living thing. My sire!

My father, I thought, *must be among the greatest of Belgians.*

* 3 *

He blocked our path. "Step aside," he ordered the filly.

She took off for the far end of the pasture.

The stallion rammed his shoulder hard into mine. "Walk with me, son. I only visit this farm in the summer to breed, but today I was let into pasture earlier than usual — a mistake. But, while I'm here, let me tell you something."

I moved in closer to my sire. *One day,* I thought, *I will be just like him.* He stared off toward the horizon. He didn't graze the clover or notice the butterflies. I nibbled dandelion leaves and waited to hear the reason for his visit. *What did I need to know?*

"By now, the yearlings have usually already gone. Still I'm not supposed to be in your field until tomorrow. So we haven't much time before they remove me." The great Belgian snorted loud like thunder and nodded toward the mares below us. "Which is your dam?"

I whinnied toward Mamere, who stood apart from the others.

"Ah, Tina. We are old friends. Your mother has lived here for many years. She's the leader when I'm gone," he said. "She is lovely."

I sunk deep into my hooves and stretched my head high, as if I were the tallest lodgepole pine of the forest, with roots to anchor me to the earth and limbs to scale the clouds. I reached up, up, up but fell short of the stallion's withers; still I found the courage to correct him. "Mamere's the leader all of the time," I said. "This is her herd."

"Do you know who you're speaking with, young colt?"

"Yes, you're my sire. Mamere told me I will grow big like you. She says I will be a very great Belgian someday," I said.

"And, little king, what do you think it means to be great?" he asked me.

I puffed my chest far, far out. "It means everyone looks up to me most of all, that every filly and colt and mare serves me." I stomped my foot. "That I get to eat first and do whatever I want."

He said, "It's true; you were bred a fine Belgian. And I have seen you playing with your siblings and cousins today, and you are fast and strong, but being king is not a game."

The great stallion set his gaze upon Mamere's herd. He lifted his head into the wind, and I did so, too. He trotted back and forth across the hilltop, all the while watching the mares and yearlings. I tried to keep up but tired quickly.

"What did you want to tell me?" I couldn't wait any longer.

The stallion stopped suddenly and snorted. He held me there under his fiery stare, and then he said, "You need to learn your place, young one, and your place is not here. When I'm here, this is *my* herd. Not yours. Not Tina's."

I scraped the grass, and then a dandelion blossom, white and hairy, tickled my nose so deep that I sneezed it away into a hundred flying pieces.

The Belgian sniffed the wind, then whinnied toward the mares. They hardly noticed him prancing along the hilltop.

"Have they forgotten me, too?" he said to himself. "These mares have forgotten me just like the world has forgotten the draft horse."

"Forgotten? How could anyone forget about us?" I asked.

"You don't even know who you are, little horse. Who we are. We are descended from the Great Horse of Flanders. We are warhorses, nation builders, movers of mountain and forest. We were. We are coming to the end, though, I fear." Then, without a nicker or a whinny, and before I could ask him anything more, the stallion galloped away. I could not stay with him even for a stride.

I returned, alone, to my high spot on the hill, hoping the butterfly would return to distract me.

Tangles filled my belly, knotting me up so that I could not graze but could only wonder: *What did the stallion mean about all of us being forgotten? And how can I find my place?*

CHAPTER TWO

The Battle

All that afternoon, the stallion watched Mamere from where he hid behind the run-in. Janey still hadn't returned, so no one had removed him from our field. Mamere turned fierce when he came too near. He bit and charged at the mares and tried to corral the fillies, but Mamere protected all of us from him. She led the mares and yearlings to the bilberry patch growing through the south fence to keep them safe from the stallion.

In response, he kicked. He bucked. He smelled the sky and bared his teeth, then bit at the air around him, and then he charged toward the herd. "I am the king of this field," he proclaimed.

With a sudden, piercing scream, Mamere turned and made him stop. He craned his neck to sniff Mamere's flank.

The other mares lifted their heads from the lush grass and stood alert. The fillies squeezed closer in behind their own dams. The very trees around us seemed to freeze, for even the always-constant wind had fled our field.

Then the stillness in the pasture gave way to a battle. The stallion launched a strike to take over the field, so he would be in charge instead of Mamere. He wanted to breed and eat whenever he wanted. But Mamere would not give in. She was going to fight him for the good of the herd. As Mamere and the stallion fought, a dust cloud swallowed them up.

Janey was nowhere to help us. The mares and fillies and colts didn't dare help. No one did.

So I raced into the battle and ran to my dam's side. A fire like I had never felt before burned in me. I couldn't stop myself; I reared, ready to fight the stallion to my death or his. Already, he looked lathered and winded from Mamere's attack, so I struck his haunch, which was as high as I could reach.

He spun around to find that it was I—only a silly colt—who had drawn his blood. From a slender, open gash, blood trickled down his hindquarters. I brandished my front hooves and moved to strike again, but suddenly Mamere folded me into her.

The stallion stared at us. "Your dam was almost right. Centuries ago you would have been a great horse, but you will be forgotten, too—a Belgian draft made for humanity but without any purpose and with no guarantee of love. The world has almost forgotten us. All of us. If you don't find your purpose, son, you'll end up like me."

"I will never be like you. And I will forget you tomorrow."

"No, you will remember me, and now you will remember what I've said." Then the stallion nibbled at me as if he were savoring a tasty morsel of red clover. When his searching lips found the soft fine place he was seeking, he plucked off the very end-tip of my ear in an instant—before Mamere or I even knew what he had done.

A pain, radiant and sharp, filled the newly vacant space, yet I stood beside Mamere and preened my chest, as if it had never happened. A rivulet of blood ran down from the missing place onto my cheek. The stallion spit my ear bit onto the ground.

Then he walked, alone, to the corner of the pasture. The mares and foals gathered near Mamere, and I began to tremble.

"My darling?" Mamere whispered.

I leaned in close to her.

"You *will* make a very great horse. And I will remember what you did this day." Mamere blew onto my ear, then lay down in the grass to rest.

Later that evening, Janey returned to the barn and removed the stallion and our field returned to peace.

CHAPTER THREE

You Are My Home

Safe again and with no need to stand guard, I dozed in the shade of the giant white spruce shuddering in the wind. Mamere grazed beside me. Though my ear throbbed, I dreamed of how I had saved her.

I stretched awake and whickered across the grass. The mares and their foals were spread across the pasture.

Even when our caretaker, Janey, entered the field with our grain, Mamere stayed by my side.

"I heard trouble found your colt yesterday. Let me get a look at him," Janey said. She flung her hands in my dam's face to drive Mamere away. "Go on, Tina!"

Mamere flattened her ears at Janey, and the woman only laughed. "Missy, I know you can't be pinning your pretty ears at me. All I do is dote on you. You've been my best mare for fifteen years." Before Janey could examine me, she saw all the cuts and swollen places and hoofprints on my mother — hoofprints from the stallion.

"What happened to you? Let me see, girl."

My dam turn the swollen side of her face toward Janey. The sight of her best mare covered with bruises and her left eye swollen shut made Janey pull back.

"Oh, boy. Why did I let anyone else handle the stallion?"

Then she noticed my now-cleft ear and reached out to touch it. I twitched her hand away.

"Decided to take on big daddy, did you? Handsome, but not the smartest cookie in the jar, I think." She rubbed away dried blood from my cheek and neck.

"You picked a lousy time to fight a stallion, I'll tell you that. Now you're deformed! You've lost the tip of your ear. We'll just hope that won't matter. You're still a nearly perfect colt," Janey said, then she ran her fingers through my forelock. "All right, stop pouting; I admire your courage, little one. I'd keep you for my own if I could."

Janey tickled my mouth, and Mamere nudged my head up.

"Besides," Janey said. "Some very fine people have gone missing a bit of their ear, you know. Van Gogh comes first to mind." Janey patted my neck. "My favorite artist, Van Gogh. We could name you after one of his paintings. Hmmm . . . so many to choose from, aren't there? We could call you Marcelle, after *The Baby Marcelle*. No, no, that won't do. You're a Belgian; you won't be a baby forever. I suppose you might like to be called *Basket of Apples,* or would you rather eat a basket of apples?"

She smiled at me and scratched my neck. "I've got it now. *Cypress!* Van Gogh loved to paint the cypress. If I could, I would name you Cypress. I will miss you, sweet one." Janey sighed.

Where is Janey going now? I wondered.

Janey kissed my head and started toward the barn. I spurred a long breath across the ground. The sugary dew at dawn made morning grazing ever so sweet, but my nagging dreams of the stallion had a stronger hold on me than breakfast.

"Mamere," I asked, "why did my father let me win?"

She tugged at the fescue but kept quiet. I nipped at her shoulder until she answered me.

"Because the legacy of our breed lives on in colts like you. Even the stallion, with all his strength and courage, grieves that we have lost our place in the world, and still, even he has hope that we will be restored. Your sire could not fight his own son to the death. You, and all the yearlings, are his living hope. He could not kill you."

"I don't want to be the stallion's son. He's mean and no one likes him."

Mamere nuzzled me. "My darling, you are my son, too. You acted quickly and with fierce courage when our herd was under attack."

"He told me that all the yearlings are usually gone when he comes here. Where do we go?"

My dam grazed without answering me. She would not even look up or whicker or nuzzle. I had never seen Mamere so withdrawn from me or the herd. The sun breached the hilltop, silhouetting the fillies and colts gathered there.

"He said I need to find my place—isn't my place here?" I stomped the ground and demanded that she respond.

But she only said, "Child, run along. The day is getting away from you. Enjoy the sunshine and run in the wind with your friends. We will talk tonight."

Since I had fought the stallion, the other foals wouldn't race me. The colts only pretended to contest the highest spot on the rock, and the fillies hardly put up a good fight.

When I swished my tail to bother away a horsefly, a small cabbage butterfly — the same one from before, I thought — flew off, too. Right away I saw that her right wing now had its pure-white tip torn and ripped.

She should have been resting her broken wing beneath the shade of a tree. Yet she busily spiraled around me, then touched down lightly on my withers. I worried the sunshine might scorch her, so I turned to make her some shade. I stood as still as I could while she rested. She fluttered up and settled near my cleft ear, and then I remembered the stallion, again.

All day instead of racing colts and fillies, I stayed with the butterfly. At last, when the great horned owl awoke to take his hunting post in the old dead pine, the ivory butterfly vanished into the night. And I raced down the hill to Mamere.

"Mamere!" I called out as I galloped down to her. "Mamere! Today I met a butterfly with a broken wing, just like my ear. And I helped her!"

She nickered me quiet while she inspected my ear.

"Tomorrow I will help her again!" I shouted. "I'll spend the entire summer finding nectar and shade and places for her to rest."

"Helping others is what makes you great. That's your purpose. Believe in that for all your life."

Then Mamere spoke somberly. "Come near to me; stand close, like you did when you were a much smaller colt. One day you will grow even taller than I am, my sweetest." And her voice grew quiet.

She bent down to nuzzle me, and her breath smelled of sweet molasses. "Let me tell you a story I have told too many times. Yes, I know where you are going. Tomorrow, you will leave me. Not just for a day, or a week, but to start a new life in a new place.

"Darling, you were bred to help every living creature. Service is the way of the draft. Your life's work is to serve and to please, to heal when you can, and to bring a gentle peace to those in need—whomever and wherever they are."

"Like the hurt butterfly?"

"Yes, that's right. All Belgians were born for this reason," Mamere said.

"All of them?"

"Yes, me and the dams. The colts and the fillies. And your cousins and brothers and sisters. Even your father, though it seems he has lost his way."

I pranced in circles around my dam. "Really? I have other brothers and sisters? Am I your favorite?"

"I love you all, of course."

I rammed into her side.

Mamere nickered me to stop, but I did not. "Am I the fastest of your children?"

She stayed quiet, so I butted into her again, and this time she gave in to my game.

"Oh, yes, you are most definitely the fastest," she agreed.

"Am I the biggest?" I charged my dam, and just as I reached her, Mamere stepped aside. I sprawled down into the grass.

"Well, you are quite large, yes," Mamere whickered.

I liked knowing that I was the biggest and fastest of all.

"But am I the best at helping? I know I must be."

Mamere pulled me close, so, so close that I could hardly breathe. "You are my sweetest; yes, you are. Now, listen; tomorrow you may well find a new place to serve." Then she turned away.

"Please, tell me. What will happen to me?"

"This is the way it must be," she said. "This is the purpose for which we have been bred: to leave here and go out into the world. Despite what your father thinks, the world still needs us. Janey says that most of our yearlings go on to fine homes."

"Not all of them?"

She nuzzled me. "Tomorrow, you will find a new home. Your help is needed elsewhere. Do you understand?"

I rested my head on my dam and rumbled. She had taught me to be an honest horse, for that is an honored trait of all Belgians. "No, I don't understand," I answered. My lip quivered and I tried to hide in her mane.

"Tomorrow you will be sold at auction. A sale of the finest drafts from all around. After that?" Mamere blew her still-sweet breath across my face. "You must accept whatever the day brings." She tried to comfort me. "I only know what Janey tells me, and what I hear when she returns from the auction house. Often, she speaks of kindly people; occasionally, she weeps."

"How many children of yours have gone to the auction?"

"Oh, my son, too many. I imagine the end of my service here is approaching. Even a broodmare's work can't last forever. Janey has been reducing the herd these past few years. There will be a price to pay for your father's appearance in our field yesterday. I expect we've missed our breeding time for this season. That will cost Janey dearly. I may only have another season or two left with her."

Mamere looked out at the dark and distant mountains—solemn giants surrounding our field. She blew out across my face, trying to comfort me, but the sadness inside her escaped. Her breath hinted at sorrow or regret or change in fortune.

"Will you go to the auction house, too? When you leave here?" I asked.

"What a kind colt you are to worry about me. All right, yes, you are my favorite." Mamere nudged me away, but I stayed tucked in. "Run on, now," she urged me. "Look at all of your cousins playing without you."

The other yearlings were galloping through the field, but I stayed with Mamere, and we watched the sparkling stars ignite and race across the sky.

After a long quiet, my dam dreamed aloud, "I do wish . . ."

"What do you wish?" I needed to know.

The brightest star of the night flared close and lit up Mamere's face. "Darling, I wish that you will always, for the rest of your life, have fields to run in, mountains to protect you, and stars to gaze upon. That is all. Now, go on and catch up," Mamere insisted.

I stood still and asked, "Why must I go? This is my place."

My dam whickered. "Your father was right about this: no horse stays here forever, gentle one. Not even I. This place is for making horses, not for keeping them."

I reached up to catch Mamere's breath and make it my own. I breathed in all the hope and power and magic of every shooting star in the night sky. I sent a new promise back to her and said again, "My place is with you. Do you know what I wish?"

She sighed, relaxing against me. "Sweetest, you

are too young to know what you really wish, but go on, tell me."

I touched my muzzle to Mamere's. "Here is my wish: wherever I go tomorrow, I wish for you to go there with me so that I won't be lonely and you won't be alone."

"Yours is a very generous heart, indeed, and these stars tonight are strong. Yes, then, my sweetest, my biggest, my fastest, and my favorite one! May our two wishes come to pass, and may tomorrow find us together."

I curled up in the grass with Mamere to watch for our tomorrow. From the branches of the pine, I heard the owl's wings beat, felt its hunting eyes pierce the night, and then heard the cottontail's last squeak. I moved still closer to my dam as the darkness moved closer, too.

CHAPTER FOUR

One Last Wish

Before the sun came up, Janey came with breakfast. Mamere urged me to eat my grain, and she gave me hers. "We have a few minutes more. Today you'll need your strength and energy. Eat."

Janey reached her hand to touch Mamere's face. "Tina, there's not another like you."

Janey nudged her floppy straw hat out of her eyes and sighed. "Time to go."

One last star raced across the August sky. I looked up and pleaded, again, with the wishing stars. *Please keep me with Mamere for today and tomorrow and tomorrow.*

"Come on, Cypress. Time to go." Janey said.

Mamere pushed at my barrel with her muzzle. I stomped and started to kick out. I wanted to bolt away to the top of my hill, but I hadn't a chance. I pushed my feet into the ground. I refused to walk on.

"Mamere, no! I won't go. We're supposed to stay together. Please, Mamere. Don't make me go," I pleaded.

From hiding, in the dark of morning, two farmhands appeared. One haltered me; and the other, Mamere. In seconds, they forced both of us into the black cavern of the trailer.

"Mamere! No! What is happening?"

"We are going to auction. Your wish came true. We are going together," she said.

Janey and the hands loaded the other foals next. Mamere whinnied to all of us. "Remember your calling and never give up! You are all purebred Belgians. Made to work and to serve. This is only your beginning. Do not be afraid."

I tried to be brave and believe Mamere, but it was the stallion's words I thought of: *We are coming to the end, I fear.* I shuddered to think that my father could be right.

CHAPTER FIVE

Nothing of Value

Even though I was with Mamere, I was afraid of what might happen. The trailer was dark and cold and I was tied in place. I couldn't nuzzle her or curl up next to her.

Tangles started to trace their way along my barrel, looking for a way inside, or looking for a way out. I could not tell; I could only want them to stop. I kicked and pawed at myself and made a racket to quiet the tangles.

Mamere brought me back from their deathly grip. "Hush, there is so much to tell you." She bent her head to me. "We will be there soon. Now, listen closely with your ears; listen also with your mind and your heart. I've heard Janey and the farmhands describe this sale many times. While I don't know what will happen, I do know this: it is always in a horse's best interest to stay alert and be aware."

"Alert so I can help? Like when I helped the butterfly and when I helped you?"

"At the auction, you will need to help yourself first. Everything around you is an opportunity. You must watch for just the right one. When Janey's grandchildren have come to our farm, I've seen how their hearts are open and kind toward the horses in a way that is different even from Janey. So, reach out to children, if you see any. Look into the eyes of any man or woman who appears kind."

"But Mamere, I will have you with me."

"But if we should get separated, stay to yourself, and, perhaps, you'll be noticed. If you get hit, accept the beating no matter how harsh. You may feel frightened; act brave! You mustn't give up."

There was no way to run, so I crouched my whole trembling self between Mamere and the trailer wall.

When, at last, we arrived at the auction, Janey told the grader that I was the finest Belgian she had ever bred, but he did not see me through Janey's eyes.

"Not good enough!" he shouted. "Bad ear!"

He ordered workers to take the other colts and fillies and Mamere to the opposite end of the building, where the sale of fine horses was starting. My father had left his mark on me, and this mark — the missing tip of my ear — made the man cast me off.

Good Janey didn't budge. She held me aside to appeal the grader's choice, and we waited while he inspected my papers.

I pulled to go with my dam. *My place is with Mamere.* I tried to tell Janey by yanking against the lead. Then I found my voice and whinnied as loud as I could. No one called back, not even Mamere, who stood quietly with one of Janey's helpers, waiting. Janey begged me to quiet down.

My papers, proof of my lineage, would not change the grader's mind. "No, he can't go to the yearling sale," he said.

"What?" Janey blew up at the grader. "You're sending him to the kill sale?"

I reared and yanked hard on the lead rope to escape to the trailer or any place away from there.

"Mamere, help me!"

My dam said nothing. She would not move a foot nor an ear, but she showed the whites of her eyes. That was the first time I had seen her afraid.

But Janey turned dark in the face; she stamped her feet and shook her hat. "I will not let this horse get butchered—ground up—because you don't know a good colt from pet food. You're a blooming idiot. Now, let him go with my other foals!"

"Forget it, lady. Move on." The grader folded his glasses and rubbed his nose. Without another word, he tore my papers to pieces, leaving Janey holding nothing of value, holding only me.

"You can't do that! You can't do that!" Janey hollered. She tossed her hat on the dusty ground.

"I just did; he's going over there. Now, move; you're holding up my line!"

Janey lowered her voice from a yell to a plea. "Sir, please. Forgive me. He is a fine and good animal; he deserves something more. Please, can the mare at least go with him?"

The grader looked at the line forming, then at his watch. Janey didn't budge. Finally, he waved the auction workmen over to remove Mamere and me. We walked on to the kill sale; we walked on together and joined the other forgotten horses.

CHAPTER SIX

To the Kill Sale

A skinny man carrying a long stick corralled us into a maze of cold gates and steel fences. He took us from Janey and away from the foals.

When I resisted, he struck me with his prod. "Come on, get in here," he yelled.

Janey ran up beside me. "Little man, be good," she said. "No funny antics."

Standing there in the crowded chaos, Janey covered her face with her hands. Perhaps she had grown tired of bringing her Belgians to auction.

She wiped her eyes on her sleeve and spoke to herself. "Stop it! Stop it, Jane. Get hold of yourself. You do your best; that's all you can do." She kissed the top of my head and patted Mamere's neck. Then, there was no one left to help us, and I never saw Janey again.

Through every sharp turn of the corral, the stick man poked at my barrel and tapped at my neck to keep me moving. I didn't strike back, nor did I complain, nor did Mamere. Both of us obeyed, at first. I tried to suckle Mamere, and the man beat me away.

He kept us moving to the kill sale.

I thought of my dam's story of the special calling of our breed: to help. "Mamere, I can save us. I will help us both."

"Oh, sweet one, you may have wished the wrong wish, to be bound to me. Had you been sent in with the yearlings, you'd have a chance of finding a good home, but who will want an old broodmare and her son? Who but a kill buyer will have need of a tired mare and a colt with no papers?"

"Shhh, we're together now, and we'll stay together, Mamere."

I stepped to the front of the pen. I sought out women, children, and kind-faced men. I only needed to find but one true friend.

I stretched my neck between the corral bars and nickered to everyone who passed by. Soon, a crowd gathered. Some wanted to look at my teeth; others handled me in places that even Mamere had avoided.

In the commotion, I glimpsed people whom I would willingly serve and gladly befriend, but the stick man always made me move away from them. Little by little, I could see Mamere giving up hope.

A fine lady strolled by with her arm sealed in a hard cast. I called her over, then reached through the bars toward her. She laughed with the delightful, dainty laugh of a wren.

"You're a smart one and quite right. I found a bit of trouble. Thank you for checking on me," she said.

The lady patted my neck. "Oh, a gentle giant— what a breed! I probably need a Belgian like you, boy." She practically nickered, so I nickered, too. "If I had a calm horse, a good horse to take care of me, a horse I could count on, well, then . . . wouldn't that be fine!"

I enjoyed this lady's gentle voice and imagined her calling me in for grain each morning. I closed my eyes and nuzzled her when she came close. With her good arm, she fluffed my forelock, then asked, "Is he selling on his own?"

The stick man shook his head. "This lot is going up as one. If you want him, gotta bid on 'em both."

The pretty lady kissed my cheek. "Oh, sweet Belgian, today is not your day. If it were just you, I'd take you home right now and save you the indignity of this place. I'm so sorry. I have no need for a mare."

I whinnied good-bye to the lady. I made welcome

room for a new hope. If we were to make it, I needed just the right someone to help us both.

Two men had been eyeing us all morning, and now they talked openly about how much they could get per pound — first for me and then also for Mamere.

"Turn away from those men," Mamere said, and she pushed me away from the two buyers leaning against the gate, watching us, encouraging each other in speculation and greed.

I couldn't help but listen. I broke away from my dam and trotted over to hear more.

"Come on, let me have this pair. I gotta leave here with some weight on the truck. These two and I'm out. I'll leave the rest for you to pick over. How 'bout it?"

"That doesn't sound like a good deal to me. It's more fun to let you bid up and then come in late and grab a couple thousand easy pounds out from under you."

The two men laughed over which of them would win my dam and me. The kill sale was about to begin; just three pens separated Mamere and me from the auction block.

I ran back to my dam.

"Here, now," she said. "Keep away. I want you with me until . . ."

"Until what, Mamere? Until the end, just like my father said?"

She thrust her muzzle into my chin, forcing my head

up. "Shhh . . . I am with you forever, my sweetest, my fastest, my most favorite son."

I surrendered to Mamere and let her lead me by the nose to a corner out of earshot. The threat of death lurked there on the other side of the rail, in those buyers bargaining for meat. Our meat. In that moment, I would not have left Mamere's side even for a promise of endless, infinite days in a field without her.

I gave in to whatever would follow—whether we would be purchased by these or other kill buyers or might somehow miraculously find our way free from the grim journey that awaited us.

CHAPTER SEVEN

John Macadoo

The auction house was crowded and loud, but a sparkly belt buckle caught my eye as a tall and wide man with no hair at all passed by. He appeared slightly bent over, as if shouldering a great load, and the bald man stopped to watch me. His furrowed brow hinted at some worry, and he rested his chin on the gate. The veins in his temples bulged out, and I thought how badly he must hurt.

I breathed out onto the man. He lifted his head; I lifted mine. When he laughed, I puffed a quick blast of air across his face.

He laughed, again. This time, his laughter came from some deep place, just as the pileated woodpecker's laugh comes from deep within the woods.

I will grow strong and broad and might carry this gentleman anywhere he pleases, I thought.

I stood still with my legs perfectly square and let my new friend imagine a life with me by his side. We watched each other for a long while, and when I felt I knew his heart, I touched his shoulder with my nose.

"You've got a nice something about you, boy," he told me. "I've had Belgians; good horses."

He, too, talked about how much I weighed, but with admiration, not how much he could get per pound.

"Look at you! A fine draft. My last Belgian grew to just over seventeen hands. You'll reach every bit of eighteen hands, for sure." He patted my neck with a soft touch.

Mamere must have sensed his goodness, too. She came nearer and stretched out her neck to meet the shiny man. He dropped his head to meet her, and my dam breathed in his out-breath.

"He's not buying for meat," she said to me. "He's— I can't be sure, but I believe he's here to rescue."

The stick man hollered over, "Wasting your time if you just want him. These two are going up in one lot —"

The kind man held up his hand and shook his head. "Nope. Trailer's about full. I won't be bidding anymore today, but these two belong on the other side of the house. Wish I'd seen them earlier."

The man turned away. He would not be rescuing us. I leaned against the corral and whinnied, begging my new friend to change his mind.

The stick man popped my withers. "Get back off of that gate!" The prod stung my skin, and I stumbled into the fence. Stick man struck me again.

I spun around fast, lost my balance, and careened into the stick man's partner. He lifted his hand to beat me, and this time, with no hope left of avoiding the kill sale, Mamere defended me. She reared up and the handler covered his face in fear.

But Mamere backed down. "No," she said to me. "I will not strike back."

"I knew this Belgian was trouble; stupidest breed on earth. Corner the mare, and I'll get the colt," yelled the stick man. He raised his arms and poised the stick in the air.

I whinnied, hoping the bald, shiny cowboy might still linger nearby. The stick man kept prodding me until I was running and lathered into a white sweat. I squealed for my life, as it was all I could think to do.

By some miracle—perhaps that star I had wished on—the shiny man did hear my calls for help, and he came to save us.

"Leave the colt alone," he ordered the stick man.

I stopped running, but the stick man immediately came toward me.

"You heard me. Leave him alone. The mare, too. I'm John Macadoo, I've bought ten other horses here today, and I want another look at these two."

Stick man angrily left the pen. The bystanders cheered, and I trotted over to kiss my friend who was neither a lady nor a small child, but a man with a golden heart, the heart of a child. He held his hand out for Mamere; she let him rub her long white blaze.

"You're a beauty. A real beauty," he said. He rubbed the top of his head, smooth like one of the balls Janey often tossed in the pasture for us to push and pull and chase. The man said to himself, "I'm crazy for Belgians. Trailer's hit its limit, but, shoot, I'm crazy for Belgians."

Mamere rumbled at him. She closed her eyes and let the man hold the full weight of her head and of what he had done. John Macadoo beat out the kill buyers; John Macadoo won us at auction.

CHAPTER EIGHT

A New Tomorrow

John Macadoo haltered Mamere and did the same to me. He tried to lead Mamere onto the trailer, where dozens of others were restless and ready to go, but suddenly she refused to join them. My dam had seen more cruelty on this one day than ever in her life.

"What if I was wrong?" she asked me. "Could I have made a mistake about this man's intentions?"

I thought of all of Mamere's children. Year after year, Mamere sent her children out into the world with a hope for tomorrow told under an August star shower. She had told all of her colts and fillies the story of the auction. Today, she had confronted the terror that all of her children had faced. She needed a different story—one that included a different sort of tomorrow for her.

I had to help Mamere before John Macadoo changed his mind and sent us back. I may never be king, but I would not desert my dam. "Mamere, let me tell you a story," I began.

She raised her head.

"Come close to me like when I was so much smaller," I said. I pushed out my chest and held my head up. There was no fire in my eyes or steam from my muzzle, only love for her in my heart. She walked toward me, her eyes and head hanging low in defeat. I wrapped my neck around her, as best I could.

I told her how our new owner said he had come to Alberta with a mission to save horses by bringing us back to his home in Virginia, where he hoped to find us good homes. Mamere lifted her head.

"Look at him," said John Macadoo. "He's taking care of the mare. Let the colt load her; watch him. He's a little alpha."

Mamere took two steps up, and I stayed right beside her.

"I would never in a million years believe this," said one of the handlers. "The colt *is* leading her."

My dam tossed her head, and she told the new story with me. "We will face adversity, and we will face it together. We will be brave, and we mustn't give up."

I nudged Mamere up to the trailer, until I could take her no farther. Only she — she alone — could take this last, great step. Mamere looked back at me.

"Tell me something more, my courageous son," she said.

Two men stood at each side of the trailer. Mamere kept a bittersweet silence while she decided whether to go on her own or be broken into submission.

I looked back at the auction. The chutes stood empty of all yearlings. Soon enough, they would be full of more colts and more fillies. For a springtime and a summer, they would all race inside the fences by the mountains. In a new season, a different colt might play pretend king. Beyond the auction house, I gazed one last time upon the Alberta mountains.

"Mamere, walk on. While we have this chance, walk on and I will, too."

There is something to be said for having a purpose. A horse on his way to slaughter has a purpose: to endure suffering and torture so that man or animal may eat. Surrendering your life for the nourishment of God's creatures is a noble purpose. But, such a purpose was not for me, not for my dam, not that day.

Mamere stepped into the trailer, and she did not look back. I whinnied good-bye to Alberta. We set off with John Macadoo, wearing halters with his name on them, packed tightly in a trailer and headed for a new life in Virginia.

CHAPTER NINE

Arrival and Departure

On our second day in Virginia, I heard, then saw, a child. And he saw me. An old man, using a cane to steady himself, walked beside the boy. He rested against the wood whenever he stopped. He walked with a limp, yet managed to almost keep up with the boy, who came running up to me.

"Poppa, look, a pony! Come with me!" The boy, who had curly red hair, ran in circles, then raced past John Macadoo.

"Slow down, Izzy, wait for me," his poppa shouted.

Izzy. The boy reached me first, then the man. Out of breath from trying to catch the child, he corrected the boy, "That's a colt, Izzy. A Belgian, I believe. What a breed—half love, half work! He'll be a very big and very fine horse one day. He's like you, Izzy; he's big for his age."

John Macadoo came into my field and haltered me while the older gentleman introduced himself.

"Young man, I called you earlier today. My good friend Russ Ramsey says you've brought back some nice horses from the draft sale in Alberta," he said to John Macadoo. "But allow me to introduce myself. Harry Isler from over in Buena Vista. And this is my grandson, Isler. He goes by Izzy."

John Macadoo nodded and said, "Judge Isler, good to meet you again. I believe I was in your courtroom when I was a teenager. Driving too fast." Then he asked the boy, "How old are you, Izzy? About twelve?"

"No, sir," Izzy answered. "I'm only nine, but I'm almost ten."

"Well, you sure are tall. Would you like me to bring the colt out so you can get a better look at him, Judge Isler?"

Izzy answered before his poppa could. "Oh, please, bring him out!"

John Macadoo led me out of the paddock and over to the boy and his grandfather.

I spurred a quiet puff of air on the older man's wrist. He patted my neck and Izzy did, too. The thick calluses

I felt on the pad of the judge's hand told me that he worked hard every day. The soft, quiet manner in which he handled me told me that he loved horses.

"You're not afraid of the colt, son?"

"No, Poppa. He's not afraid of me either."

The judge said to John Macadoo, "I'd like to purchase this Belgian colt."

John Macadoo forced a smile. "What's your intention, Judge Isler, if you don't mind my asking? This colt is finely bred. Even though I don't have his papers, I know he's purebred. He needs a home that appreciates him and that understands the breed."

Izzy's poppa nodded. "I'll definitely use him on the trail when he's ready; possibly train him as a hunter. We're horse people—well, Izzy will be soon, I hope."

"You know, I bought this one and his mother intending to keep them together. If I'm going to let the colt go, I want to know that he'll be well cared for. Belgians need a job, you know. If you treat him right, you'll find his heart is as strong as his work ethic. Do you have enough work for him?" John Macadoo asked.

Then, placing his hand gently on the back of the boy's head, the judge turned to the boy. "Izzy, I want you to feel like Cedarmont is your home as much as it is mine and as much as it was your mother's when she was growing up. I know you miss her very much. I do, too.

I can tell you for sure that there's no better friend than a man's horse and no better salve for his grieving heart. What do you think?"

Izzy wrapped his arms around his poppa. "Thank you so much. I love him already."

I hadn't an extra day or an hour but only a few minutes in the field to say good-bye to Mamere while John Macadoo and Izzy's poppa finished their business of exchanging me.

My Alberta wish had seen us through the auction together. Now, though, we would live apart. Mamere would stay with John Macadoo, and I would go with Izzy and his poppa.

Mamere closed her eyes, and I closed mine. For a moment, I wished us back to Alberta, when my ear was still whole, and I didn't know any of Mamere's stories. When I opened my eyes I was ready.

"Oh, Mamere. I'm leaving soon. I thought I would be here with you forever."

"Sweetest one, I've lived my entire life in fear of tomorrow. You helped me see that there is only today. How many todays have I been granted because of you? Your wish came true, and now you must let your work be your joy, my darling."

"What if I don't want to? I don't think I like the Belgian way."

Mamere flicked at my heart with her tail. "My precious child, I am right here, always. You are made from me; I am always a part of you. Be brave."

"Oh, Mamere." I blew onto her. "I will miss you."

For the last time, I found Mamere's breath and returned her one of mine.

"Turn away, now, my favorite son. Walk on," she urged me. "Wherever you go, that is where you are needed. You are a Belgian, born to serve, born to heal, and to bring a gentle peace to those in need. Remember who you are and you will never be forgotten. Walk on, son."

The sun touched Mamere's poll and crowned her with its golden light. John Macadoo slipped my halter over my head and loaded me into the small trailer that Poppa and Izzy had brought. I had hardly arrived at John Macadoo's before I departed, bound for a different farm in Virginia.

CHAPTER TEN

Cedarmont

I arrived at Cedarmont Farm, home to Izzy and Poppa. Poppa led me toward the barn downhill from the house. While keeping a loose hold on me, he opened the gate and turned me out, alone in the empty paddock directly behind the barn. Tall grass and white clover filled the small pasture.

"Here you are, boy. This is your field for now, just until you get comfortable at Cedarmont. I call this the salad bar, but don't overeat in here with all this grass!"

From my small field, I could see the house and the barn, both painted white. I couldn't see other horses but heard them eating and kicking and clanging their grain buckets against the barn walls. Were they Belgians, too?

I stood atop the boulder in my paddock. Cedarmont Farm covered the earth for as I far as I could see. Fields to run in and downy blue mountains to gaze upon surrounded me. I had been given a new home by a kind sir and a small child.

But, it was a home without Mamere.

Withdrawal is not the natural state of horses. Equines need to belong. We are whole when we are part of the whole. But, without a herd — or Mamere — I withdrew.

I had never grazed or stood without Mamere nearby. Even breathing was hard without her.

I paced the fence line up and down, calling and whinnying for her, and it did no good. I refused the grain and hay and water the boy and the old man offered me. And I left the salad bar untouched.

The coils inside a horse are many, and the tangles know the fastest way to bring a horse down. I dropped to my knees and lay down. *How could I go on without Mamere?*

"Is he colicking, Poppa? Help him!" Izzy cried.

Poppa walked to me. In his limp, I saw that he knew something of pain, too. He dropped his cane and knelt beside me. "Let me help you," he said. He lightly pressed his hand on my belly. "Hard as a rock. Here,

Izzy, use my phone to call Doctor Russ. Your colt's bowels are twisting, and nothing can get through. I'll keep him moving until the vet arrives." Poppa and Izzy led me around and around the field.

"Why do we have to keep him walking, Poppa?" Izzy asked.

"He's in extreme pain. If his intestines are tangled, they'll remain that way if he stays down. Keeping him walking gives his gut a chance to untwist and let everything pass."

Finally, the tangles did subside. Doctor Russ, the vet, arrived, just as my stool started to move. The doctor put his bare ear to my side. "Lots going on in there. That's a good sign," he observed.

"What do you mean?" Izzy asked. "Can I hear, too?"

Doctor Russ handed Izzy an instrument made for listening. "Try my stethoscope. Now, move it up and down your colt's barrel. What you're listening for is silence."

"I hear gurgles and growls."

"Yes, sir, that's what I hear, too. I didn't even need the stethoscope. That's the sound of a happy horse. No distress in there. Now, if you didn't hear any of those loud noises, know what you'd be hearing?"

Izzy shook his head.

"Blockage. Silence in a horse's gut is the sound of blockage. You did the right thing to get him moving. Keep an eye on him. Make sure he gets plenty of fresh water and starts eating normally," Doctor Russ instructed.

After that, Izzy came to my paddock night and day to help me adjust to this new life in a place far away from everything I had ever known.

Some people are like horses, made for joining up with another. Made for belonging. On my second day at Cedarmont, Izzy followed me around for the entire morning. He didn't let me out of his sight.

I let the child come near me.

"I see you," he said, and reached out his hand.

When Izzy held his palm open to me, I saw it was empty and felt it was full. Full of love and friendship.

He said softly, "It's okay, boy."

I believed him. Izzy moved slowly. He advanced one step and lowered his head. He looked down, and when he did I instinctively relaxed my desire to run—a desire that's always close by. I gave slightly toward him.

He came close enough for me to hear his breath, but not near enough for me to give him mine. Again, he offered his hand, empty of grain, but with a lingering sweetness of fresh hay or oats and kindness.

I waited beneath the old, broad cedar and pretended to graze, though the ground around the tree's roots offered nothing grazeable. I pretended to nibble at granite, dry needles, and black ants. I nibbled at the nothing, and Izzy came closer.

When I retreated, Izzy did, too. I stepped back. One left, one right, one left. The boy did the same. He walked back three steps and looked at the ground. I rumbled soft gratitude.

We were speaking. We were sharing a language. He knew me. I knew him. From the beginning, then, it was Izzy and me.

I stepped out from behind the cedar. I asked myself which would take the most courage: to flee, to run off? Or, would it be braver to lower my head to the boy's shoulder and follow him? Izzy walked up to me, and I let him clip a lead to my halter.

"I know your name," said Izzy. "It's right here on your halter, the one you were wearing when we bought you." He pointed to the nameplate. "Macadoo. Says so right here."

And, with that spoken word, I had a name that would never let me forget that I had come through death, a name that would remind me of leaving Alberta with John Macadoo and Mamere.

Macadoo. The sound of my new name also bound me in service to this boy.

CHAPTER ELEVEN

In Izzy's Service

C an I just call you Mac?" Izzy asked me one day.

I kept eating, with Izzy holding me on a long rope. He apologized for not letting me graze freely. "Poppa thinks you need to get used to me and I need to get used to you. He thinks you can help me."

While Poppa rode in the mountains every day for exercise and fresh air, Izzy would stay behind at Cedarmont, content to observe in the field. "I'm practicing science, Mac, and you can help me," Izzy would say.

He may not have been a horseman yet, but Izzy had become a disciplined observer of the natural world. He carried his notebook everywhere and noticed even the smallest details of the day. In some way, I think, the natural world eased the great grief that lived inside him. Being with Izzy eased my grief, too.

For hours, until well after lunch, which we ate in the pasture, Izzy would lean against me and read his findings aloud:

"*August twenty-fourth, three p.m., Mac's field, Cedarmont Farm, Buena Vista, Virginia. Ninety-five degrees: full sun, no rain, no clouds. Lots of grass still in the salad bar. Mac likes hay, too. A green inchworm, with yellow eyes, crawls across Mac's front left hoof. Mac doesn't mind. A kingbird sitting on the wood post flies out for a bug, goes back to the post, flies out. Goes back. Poppa's roses are blooming but with black spots on the leaves. The sun has turned Mac golden.*

Birds I've seen today:

   Kingbird —|

   Wood pewee —|

   Blue jay —|

   Mockingbird —|

   Canada geese — ⊬⊬ ⊬⊬

   Downy woodpecker —|

   Carolina wren —|

   Wild turkey —||| (at the top of the hill on the other side of the fence).

   Northern bobwhite — not sure how many. I hear the call, but don't see any.

Barn swallows — too many to count flying
through the barn."

Izzy never left his field book behind, for the pasture, the mountains, the forest, and the barnyard changed by the minute, and Izzy wanted to keep record of it all.

When he moved, I followed. He'd shift his leg or blink his eye, and I, too, would move, would blink, would lift my head. I'd go left to where the grass grew long and moist; Izzy'd lean that way, too. We'd go like this, grazing, walking, standing, for a morning, an afternoon, and — I hoped — a lifetime. He was different because of me, and I was different, too.

The boy never spoke of how he lost his mother, only that he missed her like I missed Mamere. He never uttered a word of his life before Cedarmont Farm. He never wished out loud for anything else but to be standing near me, but I sensed his suffering.

There were moments in the field when a drop of grief, and sometimes more, traveled through Izzy and into me, never breaking out of either of us. Never forming a sound, a sigh, or any sign that anyone but Izzy and I could detect.

In the first months of my life at Cedarmont, Izzy and I would remain in the field for hours, alone and together, surrounded by beauty enough to draw our grief out into the open mountain air, where mourning doves lamented with us. Walking together in my paddock made us grow stronger together.

"Walk on, Mac. Walk on," Izzy would say. He knew when it was right to lead me down the shady side of our field toward the happier-sounding birds—cardinals, phoebes, bluebirds, and mockers—all reminding Izzy and me how good it felt to stand in the sunshine.

Sometimes, we would leave the field. "Walk on," he'd say, and cluck for me to follow.

The boy loved to explore the meadow. He marveled at the changing nature of our mountain home. He showed me every little thing he recognized—delicate white Queen Anne's lace, flowering blackberry vines, and raptors circling overhead.

On summer nights, when the sun and the flies were sleeping, I grazed the pasture, while Izzy gazed at the stars. Each night, my boy named the stars and their families.

"I like knowing each star's name and its home in the sky," he would say, and point out stars with names like Bear and Great Dog.

And once, I saw stars combining into the shape of a great horse. Izzy saw it, too. He rested his head on my withers. "Do you know Pegasus, Mac?" he asked me.

I nickered.

"Pegasus is a horse—a horse with wings!"

Izzy pointed up. "There! See?"

In our summer of horses and bears in the sky, Poppa tried to coax Izzy into riding—not me, for I was still a yearling. I weighed nearly one thousand pounds already, but a baby's bones are too soft for work. Besides, just walking with Izzy, being near him, learning his voice, and letting him lead me was job enough for a colt.

But Izzy was not interested in riding lessons anyway. The earth around him fascinated him more than the thought of riding instruction.

I saw what his poppa could not see. Izzy never dreamed of winning ribbons or collecting trophies. Learning about all the creatures that lived on our splendid mountain was the calling of Izzy's heart and mind.

Mamere had told me: "You are a Belgian, born to serve, to heal, and to bring a gentle peace."

To be in Izzy's service brought both of us peace. To be always within the sound of Izzy's voice was my joy. Coming to him whenever he called. Moving with him out of the sun, into the shade, and back into the sun again. Standing next to him for as long as he cared to explore the world around him, for however long he remained, helped him as well as me.

He and I were the same—motherless, now, and new to this place. Even in the absence of his words or tears, I knew the loss of his mother was the source of his suffering. His grief and mine bound us to each other.

CHAPTER TWELVE

Poppa and Job

Our carefree days of summer ended when Izzy started school. One morning after I had been at Cedarmont long enough for the moist, hot air of summer to turn dry and cool, long enough that I had grown some but not enough to reach my head over the fence where the maple branch hung nearly within reach, Poppa called me to him.

He told me, "You and Izzy have brought happiness back to Cedarmont. Watching him with you this past month, Macadoo, has given me something, too." He turned his face to the sky. "You've been through a lot. So have I. So has Izzy."

Poppa kissed me on my cheek.

"Look over there at the Allegheny Mountains"—then he swept his hand in a wide half circle to the east—"and here in our yard, you see the Blue Ridge Mountains. How lucky are we, eh? Tucked away on a little farm in the Shenandoah Valley, where every day we wake up to these mountains."

Poppa led me through a different gate to a different pasture. "Here you are, boy," he said. "No more quarantine for you. This is your new field. You're ready to become part of our little herd now. You are home."

I looked for colts and fillies to play King of the Field, but none rushed to the fence. I looked for other Belgians to play Chase and Find, but I saw no Belgians. Then something moved under the trees.

Poppa pointed to the back fence line. "See that mule up there? From now on, you'll be in here with old Job."

At the top of the field, I saw the back half of a horse-like body, swishing its tailing. He kept grazing, and by the looks of him, he mostly liked to graze, not run.

Poppa pushed me forward. "Go on, Mac. Run! Play!"

Before, I had only imagined running through the distant Alberta mountains, as the reigning Draft King of Alberta, but now, at Cedarmont Farm, as far as I could see were soft mountains and grassy fields all around. And no one but an old mule to play with me.

After Poppa turned me out and left me in the new paddock, I ran straight to the back-field cedars to greet Job. I sidled up and pretended to nibble the grass. Though the trees were letting go of their leaves and the air was turning cooler, the pasture remained full with clover and fescue. I moved a bit closer to Job and flicked my tail right in time with his. He pinned his ears and hawed. "Go away!"

The mule showed me his backside and picked at red clover.

"If I go away, will you come find me?" I asked.

"What?" Job snapped his tail. He lifted his back leg in midair and held it ready to strike.

I stepped aside. "We played this game in Alberta. I run away someplace in the field. You run after me." I pranced around Job and shook out my mane. "Ready?"

With a mouthful of clover, he hawed again. "Go away, now!"

So I galloped away, past the three oaks, all the way to the run-in. I hid out there and waited for Job. Inside, scraps of old hay were strewn about the floor, and brilliant spiderwebs spanned the ceiling. I flushed barn swallows, finches, and sparrows.

After a long while, I peered around the wall to spy on Job. He stood at the bottom of the paddock, pulling at overgrown grass from a dip in the ground.

This mule knows how to play! I thought. *He wants me to come find him!*

I charged straight for Job, then I slowed to an easy run and reared beside him. Job flattened his ears and let out a piercing screech.

Job kicked out with his back feet, so I did, too. "Again!" I urged him. "Ready?"

The mule kicked again, this time from his side, but he missed me. "See those four ducks?" he said. "Go play with them!"

I turned and charged toward the four white ducks visiting from the neighboring pond. "Hello, ducks! Macadoo, King of the Drafts, is coming your way!"

So, while I raced the birds and the breeze, Job watched over the field. "You, go play with your birds," Job would often say. "I'll stand guard." When I needed rest, he guarded me. And once, after I had spent a tiring morning flushing swallows from the run-in, leading ducks around the paddock, and avoiding the geese under the trees, Job showed his compassion as the true king of our field — a different sort of king than my father.

"Go to the north corner, near where I have been standing all morning," he told me. "There are a few blackberries still, and I have kept your birds away."

We grazed the bushes together, and Job let me be

King of the Ducks. "Strictly ceremonial title," he said. "This is still my field."

I asked my mule one day, "Have you ever walked through those mountains?"

He lifted his head as if remembering would take him there. "Many times" was all he said. He pushed his muzzle into me and nudged me toward the freshest hay.

The last of the monarch butterflies lit upon my poll and fiddled with my ear. I remembered my father's message to me, but I still didn't understand it.

"Job, do you think Izzy and Poppa will ever forget us?" I asked him.

"Do you know how long I've lived here?" He answered me before I could guess. "Twenty years. I am part of Cedarmont like that mountain is part of Cedarmont."

I grazed beside him for a long time, thinking about what he said and what my father had said, too.

"I only met my father once," I blurted out.

"Well, that makes you fortunate. Most of us never know our sires. My mother, though, was beautiful. A bay quarter horse, fifteen hands. I loved her dearly."

"My father told me that we used to help people build cities. We used to clear mountains and help men win wars. He told me we are near the end of our usefulness. That we will be forgotten."

Job walked to a new grazing spot. He showed me a patch of clover blossoms. "There *are* enough cities. Mountains should keep their trees, and peace is better than war. No, your father was mistaken. Our work today is more important than ever in our history."

"Can you tell me more about our important work, Job? I want to know everything," I said.

"In time, son. Your most important work today is to grow strong and stay gentle. The rest, you will learn in time."

I nuzzled the mule and whickered low. And I wished that my father had known a mule like Job.

CHAPTER THIRTEEN

Molly

During the fall at Cedarmont, we grazed in the field during the warmth of day and came inside for evening grain. Job had introduced me to the third of our group, a gigantic mule, even bigger than I, named Molly. Her stall was across the aisle from Job's and mine, but she rarely spoke to either of us. Not in the barn. Not from her field, where she grazed by herself.

"Molly." Job had tried to get her attention that first night in the barn. "The colt is one of us now."

The mule slowly finished eating, then turned toward the front of her stall and spoke to me. "Every horse should be so lucky to live at a place like ours—at least, for a short time. Tell me, do you love Cedarmont?" she asked.

"I love Job. I love Poppa and the splendid mountains. And I love Izzy most of all."

"Then, I should say you love Cedarmont," Molly rumbled. "Every day, we must be grateful—much more so than Poppa or even Izzy—for Job and I and especially you know how quickly our luck could change." Then she turned away and went back to licking her grain bucket.

She was so bossy and tall, as tall as Mamere, and I was a little glad that I had Job in my field and not her.

Through the wide hole in our shared wall, Job told me, "Her mother was a Rocky Mountain mare, and her father . . . her father was an American mammoth jack! That's why she's so big."

"Well, I'll grow bigger than her!" I kicked the wall hard. "I'm a Belgian!"

Job turned his backside to me and leaned against the wall to scratch himself. "I meant, she's big for a mule, son."

He set a mouthful of grain in the small space between our two stalls. I gobbled it up. He put his face close, and I puffed a breath over him.

"Macadoo," Job said. "I have seen the horse in Molly, and it is grand." He nickered.

"What's funny?" I asked.

"And I see the mule in you! Consider that a compliment." Job scratched himself again. "Not to worry, Macadoo. You and Molly'll become friends, just like you and Izzy and you and I. Molly knows everything about this place. From her I've learned new plants, new trees, and when Molly and I go up into the mountains together, I feel young again. You could learn something from her, too, you know."

I turned away from Job. *What could I learn from a cranky mule that I hadn't already learned from Mamere?*

"You might be interested in this," Job said. "Molly knows how to unlatch her stall door. That could come in handy, don't you think?"

I ignored Job and sniffed at my door.

"Now, tell me about your dam, Macadoo. Tell me what she's like."

"Even though we are apart now, I know she is still with me. Mamere was a broodmare. She saved me from the kill sale, and I saved her, too. My dam is beautiful and strong. You would like her, I think."

I looked across the aisle. Molly had her whole entire head buried in her grain bucket, licking for the very last morsel. What could I possibly learn from her?

CHAPTER FOURTEEN

Watch Closely

I might have been content to run with ducks and butterflies through our paddock, but Molly and Poppa and Izzy started playing in the riding ring next to us. Job and I watched them there between the house and the field.

Poppa had urged Izzy to learn to ride and convinced him to try by telling him that the view of the trees and birds and the whole wide world appeared different from the saddle than from the ground. "Izzy, you are a curious boy. I'm surprised you're not interested in seeing the world around you in a new way."

"How so, Poppa?"

"Come see for yourself! I promise Molly and I will keep you safe."

So, I watched Molly carry Izzy on her back and step carefully over poles set down on the ground in the shape of a wheel. After a few weeks of practice, and once Izzy loosened his grip on the reins and relaxed in the saddle, they took to the poles again, this time at the trot. Poppa showed Izzy how to let Molly bend in spirals and turn in serpentines. The mule kept one ear on Poppa and one on Izzy.

I paced up and down the fence line, calling to them. Even when I whinnied, Molly would not look away from her work. Izzy looked every time. "Hi, Mac! Watch closely, boy. Pretty soon, it'll be you and me riding."

I longed to run and spiral, too. When would it ever be time for me to carry Izzy? Trotting back and forth, I wore a hard path in the grass. Poppa, Molly, and Izzy paid no attention. I whinnied with an extra-long haw that sounded like Job, but only Job answered me. "Go on, chase away those sparrows! Go!"

Mostly, Job and the sparrows were my delight, until Poppa taught Izzy how to jump. Then, not even the song of a wren or meadowlark could deter me from watching the ring. I went back to my worn path and begged, "Let me try! Let me jump with you!"

I stomped the ground. I rammed the fence. Poppa kept me out. Even after they had finished and gone back into the barn, I waited by the ring for a long time, imagining that I was carrying Izzy over poles and fences.

Job came to get me, and, this time, he did not order me to go away. The mule swatted me with his tail—a tail so long it dragged on the ground and collected burrs and hay as he walked through the field.

"Come with me to the new grass at the top of our field," he said. "I've saved it for us, just for today."

I wanted to jump, so I ignored Job the way everyone else had ignored me. But Job was king of our field, and kings usually get what they want.

"Let's race!" Job challenged me, and he tore away up the hill.

I had no time to say *I don't feel like running;* no time to say *I feel more like jumping.* Job raced away without me. His hay belly swayed side to side as he moved from a trot to a canter. Job, the mule, was beating me to the top of our hill.

I knew what I had to do. I cantered by the three oaks, stirred up the ducks, galloped past the run-in, and beat him. I was still the fastest of the field!

"I'm Macadoo, King of the Ducks!" I said as I ran by him.

"Where are you going?" Job asked.

"I'm going to jump!"

And I did. I ran faster than I had ever run before, so fast that the white oaks blurred to my right as I passed them. When I reached the gate, I did just as I had seen Molly do. I sprang up off my hind legs, and looking straight out at the paper birch beyond the barn, I lifted myself up.

Can I reach the mountains? Will I hover in the air? I flung my legs straight up and out.

I soared right into the hot metal that burned my belly. I scrambled to untangle myself from the gate, now bent and swinging by its bottom hinge. I stood up and shook myself out.

Job reached me first. Huffing and out of breath, he said, "Go away. To the run-in. Now."

"But—I."

"Now."

My guardian gave me an order, so I galloped off and hid there, peeking from behind the shelter. At the mangled gate, Job stood, hanging his head, as if *he* had tried, but failed, to clear it. He swished his tail pitifully in unison with gate's creaky wobble. Job even gave his lip a quiver.

Poppa came out from the barn, limping to the scene without his cane and laughing out loud. I left my hiding place. I could tell he wasn't angry about the damaged fence.

Poppa nuzzled Job. "Well, you old fool. A tad jealous of Molly, are you? Or has Macadoo got you feeling young again, the way Izzy has me? I should have guessed as much." He patted the mule on the neck; then Poppa rubbed his chin. "You sure you caused all this trouble?" He looked over at me; I ate some clover.

"Mac, you're still a baby," Poppa said. "But you're getting bigger. From the size of you, I'd guess you must be nearly two now. I don't suppose a slow walk in the mountains would do you any harm. Tomorrow, we'll teach you to pony beside Job. I believe both of you boys are feeling a bit frisky and who wouldn't be, surrounded by this beauty?"

My heart raced at the thought of walking in the mountains. Job pushed his head into Poppa's hand and got a scratch behind his ear.

"Soon we'll go exploring," Poppa promised.

CHAPTER FIFTEEN

Our Splendid Mountain

Poppa soon took us all up to the mountain, like he had promised. We left by way of the unfenced back meadow. Under a cloud cover that spanned the farm, we strode through an open field. Poppa and Job and I were in front, with Poppa on Job leading me beside them. Molly and Izzy brought up the tail.

As we entered the woods, a towhee called out, so I whinnied hello. Molly called back to me, and even Job whinnied along.

"Well, all right, then," said Poppa. "Everyone accounted for? Off we go!" he said.

While Job did the work of guiding our party all through the forest, Poppa sat high in his saddle. He looked around at the sky and deep into the trees, and he sang to us of birds and flowers.

"Yellow warbler!" Poppa cried, and then a whir of wings and song flew past. "Just passing through, heading south, I imagine," Poppa said over his shoulder to Izzy.

Job was on duty so he mostly kept quiet but offered advice, now and again. "Mind your step," he warned. "Lots of holes and rocks."

"Job? Will we go to the top?" I asked.

"Shhh . . . I'm working," he said.

A redbud branch, clinging to the last of its leaves, snapped back in my face. Izzy had taught me to recognize its heart-shaped leaves. *Are redbuds all over the mountain?* I wondered. "Job, I want to see Cedarmont from the top!"

"Not yet. You're too young to make the crest."

I trotted up beside him. "Then, can we race?"

Job kicked out. "Stay behind me, now. Let me lead you."

I heard a blue jay call from way up ahead and couldn't help but break into a jog.

"You wanted to see the mountain. Slow down and look around!" Job bossed me.

"At what?" I asked him.

"See the lace ferns around your feet? See the Queen Anne lining your path? See how the goldenrod is still in bloom? Take notice of everything, Macadoo; that's your job today. Stay back, now."

When we reached the river, Poppa said to Izzy, "Now, untack Molly. We'll stay here awhile. Let her drink from the Maury River with us." He filled his hat with water and emptied it over his head.

Izzy led Molly upriver to join us. I nickered and gave her a breath.

Molly swatted at me with her tail. "I hope you learned something today, Macadoo. One day when you are old enough and strong enough, you will carry Izzy on your own. He's going to rely on you to keep him safe, to help him find his way."

I blew across the Maury River to make it ripple, and Molly did, too. Poppa unpacked his lunch and sat down on the sunny bank in the moss. Molly and Job waded upstream, under the old, tall sycamore.

I stood next to Izzy with only wind and water between us. I could have run but did not, because I was right where I was meant to be.

CHAPTER SIXTEEN

Can You See the Wind?

I had everything I needed and all that I wanted at Cedarmont. Autumn passed, each day cooler than the one before; each day darker, too. As the days turned shorter, my coat grew longer. The hair covering my cannon bone grew long and feathery. My winter coat kept me warm and mostly dry.

The sound of the school bus rolling to a squeaky stop alerted me that Izzy was home, so I was always waiting for him by the gate in our field.

Every afternoon Poppa and Izzy would come with a grain bucket and a lead rope.

As winter inched closer and the air turned colder, I looked forward to the warmth of the barn each night.

"What is Christmas, Molly?" I asked across the lane between our stalls one especially nippy morning. A hard frost covered our field; Poppa had set out extra hay.

"Christmas is a time when people sing."

"Poppa sings every day," I reminded her, and it was true. He started each morning with a song and left us each evening with one, too. I understood that people sang when they were happy, but I still did not understand Christmas.

Job explained it a different way. "People seem to enjoy one another more at Christmas. They remember all those that they love and have loved."

I hung my head out over my door and jimmied the latch loose with my nose until the handle turned freely; just how Molly had shown me. Then I pushed the door free with my head and walked over to her stall.

"Izzy promised something special for us at Christmas. How will I know when it's coming?" I wondered aloud.

"You will be patient and wait. And, you will go back to your stall right now," said Molly.

"Besides, Christmas isn't something you can see, though you can see signs of its arrival. The sky foretells Christmas at the beginning of winter, very near the darkest day," said Job.

The hardwood trees soon dropped all their leaves, and I could see through the forest. One day, Job sniffed and said, "Smell the air, Belgian, and taste it. Is it not frosty and wet?"

That night, Poppa added a fine blanket to my coat and it kept me warm like summer inside, warm enough to nudge open my window and bathe in moonlight, while I waited for Christmas to come.

"The night smells like Alberta," I said to Job as the wind whisked a paper birch leaf past my face. "Could this wind have come from where I was born, where I lived with Mamere? Just now, I thought it smelled like our old field for a minute."

"Snow is coming," Job said. "Christmas is surely near."

"I wish you had known my dam. Cedarmont is everything she wished for me."

Job placed a mouthful of grain for me in our space. "I know you miss her. I know you do."

I ate the grain without saving even a speck, then told Job, "I like to be near Izzy because when I am it feels like Mamere never left. I lean against him, and when he talks about the forest, the field, the sky, I think I feel her with me. If only I could see her again. Sometimes, it's hard to remember my dam. Sometimes, Mamere hardly seems real anymore."

Molly heard me from across the aisle. "Nonsense. Of course she is real and still with you. Macadoo, can you see the wind?"

"No, ma'am. I see where it goes, but I cannot see the wind itself, no."

"You can't feel it either, I suppose?"

"Molly, I can feel the wind! I can even smell the wind!"

"Then you're very, very sure the wind exists?"

I sniffed my hay. Izzy had started giving us alfalfa now that the grass was gone. *Mules ask odd questions,* I thought. "Yes, I am sure. I know the wind, Molly," I answered.

Molly held her head out into the night and told me, "Put your head outside, child. Do you feel a breeze now?"

"The night is still. There is no wind," I told her.

Job whickered now. "What if the wind never returns?" he asked.

I pulled back into my stall. My chest tightened. *No more wind? No more wind?* The very thought swirled a gust into my stall that lifted some pine shavings, then swished out into the night.

No more wind! These two mules couldn't trick me. "Even if I cannot see the wind, even if I cannot feel it in every second, the wind will come back," I said.

"That's right," Molly agreed. "Remember that, always."

Throughout the night, I shared memories of Mamere with Job and Molly. Job told stories about his dam, too, who loved to walk in the Maury River. And Molly told us about a girl named Charlotte who used to live at Cedarmont a long time ago.

"There hasn't been a child here—a family—in a very long time. I will never forget Charlotte. She loved me the way Izzy loves you. Oh, she and I knew this mountain even better than Poppa. Believe it or not, it was Charlotte who taught me to unlatch my stall!" Molly told us.

"What happened to Charlotte?" I asked. "Where did she go?"

"She moved away with her mother and then came in the summertime and, usually, about now for the holidays. Then she grew up and had a child of her own, and now she . . . Now Charlotte is gone."

I whickered softly to comfort Molly.

"Thank you, Macadoo. You know, Charlotte is like the wind, too. She is always here with me, always at Cedarmont. It's good for me to tell you about her. And, now you know something of Izzy's mother, too."

I whinnied. "Charlotte was Izzy's dam?"

"Oh, son, I thought you knew," Job said.

All through the night of our remembering and recalling the ones we so loved, a white cloud held Cedarmont in stillness, and we waited for the first snow to fall.

CHAPTER SEVENTEEN

Christmas

To ready Cedarmont for Christmas, Poppa hung cedar wreaths in every window and on every door of the farmhouse. Trucks delivered flowers, new furniture, and boxes of all shapes and sizes.

"Poppa has changed since Izzy, and now you, have come here, Macadoo. We haven't seen a Christmas so full of cheer and gifts in a very long time," Molly told me.

Izzy complained about having to chop and stack wood. Job and I watched over him while he worked, swishing our tails in time with each strike of his ax.

When our boy grew tired, Poppa would take over.

He broke each log in half again with a full-force swing, then loaded the wheelbarrow full and stacked the firewood into a snaking line around the house. While he loaded and unloaded the split logs, Job and I walked along with him, on our side of the fence.

I learned from listening that this was Izzy's first Christmas without his mother. He said how much he missed her. Poppa missed her, too. *Charlotte,* Poppa called her. *My Charlotte.*

Smoke poured from the two chimneys on either end of the house, and neither fireplace could keep up with the other. Yet Poppa still would not rest. He kept busy. Instead of using his cane for support, he zigged against trees and zagged toward fence posts to steady his balance. He took Molly up into the mountain, and they came out dragging a full and round red cedar.

Though the calluses on Izzy's young hands were open sores from all the work, he braided my tail one night. "Poppa taught me this," he said, and chuckled, fumbling with the rubber bands. "He said Mom always braided her fancy pony with red and green ribbons. No ribbons for you, Mac."

Izzy polished our halters and cleaned the feed room and tack room until they glistened; soon the entire barn smelled of citrus. At night, the farmhouse was aglow with candles.

The first snowfall started before breakfast. Izzy

came to feed us and break up the ice that had formed in our water buckets overnight. With the barn door open, I caught sight of the snow beginning to blanket the ground. I pushed my window wide with my nose to taste and see Christmas. I ate my grain fast and clanged the empty bucket to urge the mules to hurry.

"Molly, I saw snow! Will Christmas come today?" I kicked the floor and the wall and the stall door, too.

"Shhh . . . we'll see."

Job passed some grain over to quiet me. "Yes, I think any day now, yes," he said.

I pawed through the pine shavings all the way to the dirt until the ground felt cold on my frog. I pulled fresh shavings from the wall and set my feet on the warm, soft bedding. This time, I knocked my grain box harder, and finally, Job and Molly joined me in making a racket so Izzy would hear us and turn us out faster.

In the paddock, under the three oaks and beneath the snow, wild turkeys pecked for acorns, and, by the run-in, the Canada geese gleaned for ryegrass seeds. I stood guard with Job and watched snowflakes pile up fast and high in the curve of his back. I couldn't help but reach out for a lick. Job sent me off to the rock at the top of our field, but it wasn't as fun to eat snow off a rock.

"Mac! Macadoo? Where are you, boy?"

I whinnied and whickered and raced to the gate when Izzy came home.

Izzy ran straight to me. "Do you remember what I promised?" he asked. "Come with me! I think it's here! Poppa has our surprise in the barn."

Izzy haltered me and led me to just outside the tack room. Poppa was in there, too. I had never seen inside and was distracted by a wall filled with old, faded ribbons and trophies stacked up everywhere, even on the floor.

"Young man, who do you think won all those prizes?" Poppa sounded like he was bragging.

"Wow, Poppa, are those yours?"

"No, sir. Those are your mother's. I cannot recall a finer horsewoman than Charlotte," Poppa answered.

Izzy reached out for one of his mother's show ribbons. "These are all my mom's? She must have been an awesome rider."

"Your mother had such talent," Poppa said. "*All* those are hers. Champion, reserve champion, novice rider of the year, junior rider of the year—your mother could ride; I'm telling you. I trained her, you know. I pressured her too much, I suppose. Pressure to win, always to win. Still, when I wasn't demanding that she be perfect, we had some fine times here at Cedarmont."

Molly kicked at her stall; she wanted to go out, but Poppa kept on talking. "Every day, it seemed, we were late for dinner. Charlotte never wanted to come home. When she was about your age, your mother even slept out here with Molly some nights."

Izzy patted me and asked, "Can I sleep out here with Mac?"

Poppa put his arm around Izzy. "Tell you what. Look out the window. Can you see the black line of that dark mountain there through the snow?"

My Izzy rose up on his toes to get a good look.

Poppa said, "The whole mountain is your winter garden, Izzy. Tomorrow, you and Molly and Job and I will go out. We'll pony Mac and take him with us. What do you say?"

I felt Izzy's heart pounding. I rubbed my face against his wool jacket.

"Now," Poppa said. "Close your eyes. I know you've been waiting for this. Open." Poppa swept his hand toward the tack trunk, where a new saddle sat on top.

Izzy put his hand on my barrel and looked down at the floor. Big, silent tears dropped onto his boots.

Poppa wrinkled his face. "What? Don't you like your new saddle?"

Izzy didn't say anything at all.

"Tell me, son. What's wrong?"

"No, it's selfish. It's just . . . Well, I thought . . . maybe it would be a telescope. I just . . . Oh, never mind. I'm sorry, Poppa."

"Oh" was all Poppa said.

Izzy tried to explain. "I love Mac and I love you. I love Job and Molly, too. I do want to ride in the mountains. I want to ride Mac and Molly and Job, but I don't care about ribbons or shows or hunting. I miss Mom so much. It hurts still every day, but I'm not her and it seems like that's who you want me to be. I'm me, Poppa, not Mom."

Poppa looked confused, then pretended to smile. "You may change your mind. You're a natural, Izzy. Just like your mother was."

Izzy dropped my lead and ran from the tack room into my stall. I followed.

CHAPTER EIGHTEEN

Christmas Secrets

I found Izzy sitting down in my stall. He had wiggled his way deep into my pine bedding. He had grown taller since summertime, and his long legs stretched out across the corner.

"Thanks, Mac. I love Poppa, I really do, but he doesn't understand. He can't make me the same as Mom. I don't want to be a rider like her or a judge like Poppa. I want to be a vet like Doctor Russ and help horses, dogs, cows, and any animal who needs me."

The barn cat jumped down from the beam and into Izzy's lap.

Izzy said, "I'm tall like my mom was. I think she was even taller than Poppa, and she could make me laugh and smile even on the worst days. She played the piano; sometimes we would play together. That was the best. I keep a picture of her by my bed, so I won't ever forget her. Like I could ever forget."

I nickered in his ear. When my boy told me about his mother, I wished I could tell him about mine.

The black cat kneaded Izzy's lap and curled up small.

"Mac, can I tell you a secret? Poppa was all the family I had after Mom died. She never brought me to Cedarmont even though she grew up here. She always said Poppa drinks and drinks and that he's sick. She wanted Poppa to get better. I know my mom loved him. She kept a picture of the two of them—just like I keep a picture of her. Since I came here and since you came, too, Mac, Poppa is better."

I nuzzled the boy to let him know that he and Poppa had helped me, too. Izzy gently lifted the sleeping cat and set him down.

"Let's put the new saddle on you, Mac. See how you like it. I'll be right back." He opened my stall door, then closed it shut behind him but didn't lock it. I could have followed him without even having to unlatch my stall door. Izzy was coming right back, so instead, I munched on my last bit of fresh hay. Before I could finish, I heard Izzy's startled voice. "Whiskey," he said. "Oh, Poppa. Poppa, you promised."

I dropped my hay and went to Izzy, but he ran into the tack room and shut the door behind him. I could hear my boy crying, but Molly hadn't taught me how to open doors like the one to the tack room. So, instead, I ran for help.

CHAPTER NINETEEN

A Boy's Grief

I made a ruckus and stirred up a fuss trying to find Poppa. I galloped through the open paddock gate and around to the front lawn, not sure what had caused Izzy to withdraw from me like that.

But the house was silent. Candlelight shone through the wreathed panes. The red cedar that Molly had dragged from the mountain stood in the front window, lit up by hundreds of tiny golden lights.

I stood in the yard, whinnying over and over, until, at last, Poppa stepped into the night — without his cane or his coat.

"Macadoo! What on earth?" His breath hung heavy in the air around him.

I charged up to the porch and stomped my front hooves on the first step. I pushed against Poppa with my head.

"Whoa, big fella. What the devil's going on?"

I whinnied for him to follow me.

"Settle down, boy. Let's get you back to your stall."

Poppa didn't need to hold my mane, for I led him back to the barn. Inside, he placed his hand on my shoulder and spoke with a winded voice. "Well. Now. What's this all about?" He folded over, I think, to steady his breathing.

That's when Izzy lunged out of the tack room. He held a glass bottle and shook his head at Poppa, as if Cedarmont had been too good to be true for all of us.

Poppa struggled to stay upright. "I . . . I, Izzy. I'm out of breath. I ran with Mac from the house without my cane."

"Did you lie?" Izzy wanted to know.

Poppa shook his head.

Molly and Job stopped eating their hay. We'd never seen Poppa with a bottle but had watched him ready the house, chop a winter's worth of wood, and ride out of the forest dragging the finest Virginia cedar — all for Izzy.

Poppa stood up straight. When he breathed in, a

deep and terrible cough took over and his face turned dark.

"You promised me you would stay sober for Mac . . . for me."

Poppa spoke clearly. "I am sober, Izzy. I am."

"Then, what is this, Poppa?" Izzy shoved the bottle toward his poppa. "This is your drink. I remember. After Mom passed away, when I first came here, I found bottles just like this one everywhere, all around Cedarmont, until we got Mac. Why? Why now when everything is so good?"

Poppa rounded his shoulders and hung his head. He brought his hardworking hands to his face, then said, "Izzy, I can't explain why I didn't throw that last bottle away. I found it in the tack room yesterday when I was setting up your new saddle. I must have hidden it here some time ago—before you came, even. But I swear I have had not one drink from it. See my steady hands? Look into my clear eyes," he said.

Izzy shut his eyes; he shook his head.

I think Poppa realized that Izzy was scared. He ran his hand through his hair. "Yes, the whiskey is mine," he admitted. "I couldn't pour it out, but I didn't drink it either. I'm trying, Izzy. I'm trying."

Izzy looked up at Poppa. He started to go to him, but instead he stopped and demanded, "Is there more?"

"Yes," Poppa said.

"Get it and pour it out now."

The old man sighed and shrugged.

"Poppa, please," Izzy pleaded.

"I can't," Poppa said.

Izzy threw the whiskey bottle onto the floor. The glass shattered and the barn started to smell of spoiled corn. "We're supposed to be a family! You're supposed to take care of me and Cedarmont."

Without a jacket or hat, Izzy ran out. I wasn't sure how I could help Izzy and Poppa, but I was going to try. I followed my boy from the barn.

CHAPTER TWENTY

Lost on the Mountain

We left Poppa, Job, and Molly behind. They didn't follow. I caught up to Izzy, and we walked across the meadow and into the forest. The snow had stopped and the sky cleared just enough to let the winter sun slice through the bare sycamore trees, white like the ground now. At a boulder ledge near the Maury River, Izzy climbed onto me. I was big enough, strong enough, now to hold him for a little while.

Izzy didn't speak. I understood that he was only a child, yet had been shouldering a terrible burden—a burden I was old enough to help carry. I stood facing the mountain while Izzy poured out all his grief and anger and confusion. I thought then how wrong my father was when he told me that there is no heavy work left for the draft breeds. This work was just different. Izzy's heavy lifting had only just started, and I was his willing partner.

For a long while after his tears stopped, Izzy stayed silent and I did, too. Not grazing or even sniffing at the grass. After a bit, he lifted his head and sighed. "Thanks for coming with me, Mac. I wanted to be alone but not really."

I reached back and touched my nose to Izzy's boot, still wet from walking in the snow.

"Good boy, Mac." He patted my shoulder. "We'll just stay for a little while, until I know what to say to Poppa. I like the quiet. I like the trees and I like the sky. The mountain helps me think." His mouth softened; I could sense it. "I learned that from Poppa."

The sunshine cut in through the forest understory and shone down through the river birch onto us. I blew out to watch my breath spiral and swirl around in the last daylight.

Izzy stretched out on my back and let his legs dangle against my barrel. The two of us kept still and silent until the sun only glistened at our feet, on its way below Saddle Mountain, on the other side of Rockbridge County. Izzy slid down to lead us home. We passed an empty pine strand that Poppa had recently cleared for timber, then came to a grassy place on the side of a hill.

"Come on, boy, this is a shortcut. We cross here and we'll be back in your field in no time. Poppa showed me once." Izzy scratched his head. "I think this is the way."

I whinnied into the open and my own voice answered. I refused to go farther in the direction Izzy wanted. Izzy was wrong.

I squared up my feet and sunk them into the ground. Whether he knew it or not, Izzy needed me to get him home. A barred owl had already made its first survey-ing flight; soon there would be no sunlight left at all.

"Mac!" Izzy shouted. I only had on my halter, so Izzy yanked that as hard as he could to pull my head down. "Walk on!"

I refused. Izzy was leading us down deeper into the mountain base, away from home. I whinnied, again, and called out for help. No one called back to me. Not Molly. Not Job. I used all my strength until Izzy let go of my halter and gave in.

"All right," said Izzy. "We'll go your way."

He climbed up onto my back. I whinnied every few minutes, but Izzy and I were alone, with darkness enclosing. Izzy started to shiver. He hadn't any gloves on, but warmed his hands in my mane. I kept walking toward home, all the while whinnying for someone.

Finally, I heard a reply, but it was not a whinny or a nicker.

It was Poppa.

I followed his voice, calling out our names without stopping, until I could see the light from the house, then the light from the barn. Poppa stood waiting just in the barn doorway. Izzy slid down and ran to him.

Poppa opened his arms. "Please, Izzy," he said. "Believe me. You and our little herd are the reasons I am healthy and sober."

Izzy rested his head on Poppa's shoulder and nodded. "I was so scared without you," he said. "I'm glad to be home."

CHAPTER TWENTY-ONE

A Family at Cedarmont, Again

Over the years, the bond between Poppa and Izzy grew stronger. Poppa needed his cane all the time now, but still he kept riding every day. Izzy did turn out to be like Charlotte in one way. By the time he was thirteen, he was as tall as Poppa and still growing.

I kept busy learning all I could from Molly and Job. After I'd been at Cedarmont for several years and had reached a good height and weight, Poppa gave me the conditioning and schooling that I needed to go with Izzy. Some days we built up my strength, power, and suppleness, and on others we worked to improve my focus, attention, and discipline. Poppa praised my gentle nature, and he never asked Izzy to win a ribbon or a trophy, only to ride in the mountains like he wanted. We had become a family. Poppa, Molly, Job, and I. And we trusted one another.

The first time Izzy took me out on the trail our trust was tested. I had learned how to listen and obey the aids from Izzy. His legs, seat, and hands were stronger than words. The reins and the bit even stronger. But Poppa never taught me how Izzy's breath was an aid, too. This I learned on my own.

Early one August morning, while the air was cool but still muggy, we rode out with Poppa and Molly.

I often knew how Izzy wanted me to go, even before he asked. But part of my job was to help him learn to use his aids correctly. Still, I should have taken better care of him on our first trail ride. I had more learning to do, too.

Being out on a trail was different from our practice with Poppa in the ring. On the trail, in the forest, and in the mountain, I could hear and see and feel better than Izzy could. My mistake that day was not taking care of my boy from our first step out. The trouble started when Poppa asked if Izzy felt ready to canter.

"Yes, I know what to do. You always say that riding Mac's like riding a sofa; he'll take care of me."

"That's right, Mac is easy and safe. Now, sit deep, grab mane, pull your leg back—"

Izzy shortened my reins. He breathed a full deep

breath. I knew what would come next. He placed his calf at the girth, and then pressed his boot into my barrel to ask for the canter.

"I'm a good rider," Izzy said to himself. "I can do this."

He rose just out of the saddle, posting faster and faster, and I picked up speed with him until we were cantering.

In all the excitement of cantering on the trail, I lost sight of Poppa and Molly, so instead I followed Izzy's hands and legs. But Izzy wasn't paying attention either and soon he had steered me into a nest of long vines, thicker than the limbs of an old dogwood. Poppa and Molly had disappeared, so we stopped while Izzy tried to figure his way out.

"Poppa, come back. I can't see which way to go."

But Poppa didn't answer.

I halted and asked the mountain which way to go. Job had taught me to think of myself as part of the mountain and to pay attention to the air and the ground, the river and the sky, and to every living thing.

Izzy panicked. He took short quick breaths. He kicked at my sides, urging me forward. He pulled the reins left then right. He pressed the heel of his boot into my side, telling me to turn, then changed his mind and pulled on the reins and made the bit tight in my mouth. He wanted me to back up. He was afraid.

I blocked out all of the confusing, fearful aids from Izzy. To get him safely reunited with our family, I ignored his squirming and kicking and his fast, shallow breathing.

"Poppa, help! Where are you? What do I do?" Izzy panicked and shouted into the trees.

No answer came. Not from a mule or a blue jay or a goldfinch. With another jab to my barrel, Izzy tried to make me move again. Somehow, we had gotten turned around. Izzy didn't know which way to go.

"We're lost, Mac! What if Poppa can't find us? I don't know what to do. What if we never find him?"

If we were to find our family, I needed to take over. As long as Izzy stayed in the saddle, I could lead us. If he dismounted, Izzy would lead me or I'd have to over-take him. If I could get to the Maury River, we could find Poppa.

Straight ahead, the forest understory was a twisted, tangled mess of vines so thick that sunlight could barely pass through.

To our west, a beaver had gnawed down young hardwoods and left a jagged path of pointy stumps. The footing was loose with rocks that covered a steep cliff. Nearby a still-wet snake had coiled herself in the sun to dry. I smelled around for the dampest spot of earth.

A small copper butterfly with gossamer orange

wings flitted around us. She landed near my cleft ear and I thought of my father.

"You don't even know who you are. Who we are," he had said.

The copper fluttered up, then back down on me. I tried to twitch her away, but she clung to my ear with her dainty legs. *Remember.*

And even though I had been gelded at John Macadoo's and didn't have the blood of a stallion, there in the mountain forest I found that I could remember. "We are movers of mountain and forest," my father had also said.

With the copper's help, I realized that the beaver and the rocks and the snake were pointing the way to the Maury River. I heard tumbling water below and the *chip-chip, po-ta-to chip* of a goldfinch. We would find our family there, but we would need to go down. Straight down.

I reached back and nudged Izzy's boot to get his attention and nodded my head toward the river. Izzy picked up his reins — glad to be moving — and when he did, I walked on and took the shortest way, straight toward the cliff. Once we started, Izzy remembered to lean back, and his weight helped balance us. Izzy relaxed his hands and gave me a long rein. His breathing slowed, too, and that told me that Izzy felt surer of himself and surer of me. I headed straight for the river, keeping my eyes and nose close to the earth.

We reached the bottom safely, and Izzy let out a great sigh. Soon, we joined our family, waiting for us downstream in the shallow, rocky part of the Maury River.

When we arrived, Poppa let out a great sigh, too. "There you are, my lost loves! I was giving you five more minutes before I came looking. There's a reason I've brought Mac into the mountains with the mules so often, Izzy. Nothing startles them, and mules are smarter than people in the woods. Out here, your Belgian is almost as bright as Job or Molly. They've taught him well."

Izzy grew in skills and confidence that day. I did, too. For a moment on the trail, I thought I had lost my way until I remembered who I was. Who we were. I wondered if my father would have been proud.

CHAPTER TWENTY-TWO

The Far End of the Field

One Saturday morning in September, Izzy hurried out to our field carrying his pencils and binoculars well before Molly and Poppa left for Tamworth Springs to help train the new hunting pups. I desperately wanted to go with them and whinnied loud and often to make my wishes clear.

I could always tell when Poppa and Molly were going to hunt. Even before the season officially opened, Poppa wore his hunting jacket and best riding pants and shined his tall boots whenever the club would ride out to check fences, set courses, or practice with the pack.

Izzy gave Job and me our breakfast in the field and promised to bring us inside if the day turned too hot.

Job had never liked hunting, and as old as Molly was, she still loved to ride out with Poppa to see her friends at Tamworth Springs. The boy sat in his usual spot on the great granite slab at the top of our paddock. He wrote furiously, then read:

"September fifteenth, eight a.m., Cedarmont Farm, Buena Vista, Virginia. Eighty degrees by the barn, approximately. Mild day, cruel drought. Oak gone to seed, acorns everywhere, dogwood brittle. Pond nearly dry, no frogs seen or heard. Job and Mac drank all their water last night. They're grazing together. A beautiful day, but rain, rain, rain would make today perfect.

Butterflies I've already seen this a.m.:

> *Spicebush swallowtail rested on Mac's torn ear*
> *for a while*
> *Pipevine swallowtail*
> *Lots of coppers, a few monarchs, too*
> *Yellow swallowtail that I think may be a female*
> *spicebush of the yellow variety because she's*
> *getting lots of attention from the black one."*

We were soon captivated with the dance of the spicebush swallowtail, and as Poppa and Molly left Cedarmont for Tamworth Springs, late in the morning on this most beautiful day, Molly whinnied for me. I left Izzy and cantered along the fence as Molly and Poppa passed.

"I wish I could come with you! Maybe tomorrow

Izzy and I will ride to Tamworth Springs, too," I called after her. "Will the beagles run tomorrow? Will all the horses from all around come back tomorrow? And the man who blows the horn to start the hunt?"

Molly halted to answer me, but Poppa gave her a little kick. "Walk on, girl," he said.

She wouldn't budge. "It would make me so happy if you and Izzy could come today."

Poppa squeezed Molly behind the girth. "What's gotten into you?"

I nickered. "Tomorrow, Molly. We will come with you."

"Yes," she said. "Tomorrow." Then she trotted away.

I stood at the gate, whinnying until I was sure she was gone. When finally I heard the baying of beagles through the woods, I knew they would not return until the late afternoon.

Izzy called me back to him. "Quick, Mac! Come here!" he yelled out, and I ran to the far end of the field. "Look!" he said. "The oxeye daisy! Was it here yesterday? How could we have missed this one?" He wrote in his notebook, then read again:

"Oxeye daisy: white petals, big yellow eye, jagged leaves. More spindly than Poppa's Shasta daisy. About twelve inches high. Looks just like the Shasta's bloom. Only one plant."

I smelled the wildflower just before Job ate it.

Izzy laughed and said, "Well, I'm hungry, too, Job." Then he scribbled and read: *"Mules eat wild daisies. Not sure about Belgians."*

He folded up his notebook, sat down beside us, and pulled an apple from his sack. A generous boy, Izzy hardly got half, between biting off chunks to share with Job and with me.

Before Izzy could climb up the oldest of the three oaks to rest in its broad lower limbs, Molly exploded through the meadow, carrying Doctor Russ, the veterinarian, not Poppa. They galloped straight toward our paddock.

"Izzy, tack up Mac!" the vet instructed from the saddle. "Let's go."

"Poppa's hurt," Molly quietly told Job and me.

I stomped the ground and tossed my head. I tried to jump the gate, but fell back.

Molly touched her nose to mine. "Settle down but make haste, Macadoo. Your boy needs you."

Job pinned his ears at Molly, then turned to me. "Son, let the boy take you out of here, and let Molly lead you to the field. See how you may be of service." He breathed over me to make me brave.

Doctor Russ hurried Izzy along. "Please, Izzy. You need to tack up Mac and ride with me back to Tamworth Springs. There's been an accident."

"What's happened?" Izzy asked.

The vet, a man of girth and height just suited for a Rocky Mountain mare–mammoth jack cross, shifted his weight, side to side, in the saddle. "Izzy, your grand-dad fell. Hit his head hard. Now, he's talking a bit of nonsense. I'm afraid he may have broken his leg, too. An ambulance is on its way, but he wants to see you. We should go now."

The boy stood squinting at the sun. When Izzy still would not budge, I shoved my barrel against the gate.

Doctor Russ spoke softly to my boy. "Your poppa's tough. He'll be okay. Just trot Mac through the forest."

Izzy patted my neck. "You'll get me to him, Mac. I trust you."

He folded away his notebook and walked me to the barn. Izzy tacked me up all on his own. A hairy brown wolf spider crawled along the floor with a hundred spiderlings or more riding on her back, yet Izzy never reached for his pencil. The boy was busy summoning his courage, and I was, too.

As we passed the gelding field, on the way to Tamworth Springs, Job stood square at the gate and asked after me, "Son, you know the forest?"

I nickered.

"Then I'll stand here, right here, until you come home," Job called.

Molly led us through the woods at a fast trot. I

could've managed the hard and narrow path without Molly's help; I would have cantered the whole way to Poppa. Izzy fidgeted with his hands, then squeezed my reins too tight. He wiggled his seat and, yet, tried to reassure me. "We'll be there soon," he said. "Don't worry."

Halfway to Poppa, Doctor Russ slowed Molly down and asked, "Everything fine back there? We're going to canter now."

"I know what to do, Doctor Russ. You go, then we'll go," Izzy said.

He grabbed mane and gave me my neck. My hooves lifted off exactly in time with Molly's, and all of us cantered away.

On the field, horses stood bunched together in groups of six and three and two, and some stood alone. Most of the riders remained mounted; a few stood on the ground talking to one another. The mild day had brought out the entire hunt club, even though the opening meet was still weeks away. A group of observers — guests of the club — stood a ways off from the horses, pointing at something uphill.

The hounds that I had so often heard baying tumbled over one another in a frolic. A few pups had scampered away from the pack and followed their noses off into the brush at the edge of the field. All I could see was the tips of their white tails wagging furiously in the tall grass.

"Yip, yip, yip." The hunt master called the pups back to him. "Yip, yip, yip."

This should have been a fun day of working with the young dogs who were all yelping and playing in the field, but something had gone terribly wrong.

The kindly Doctor Russ stopped and pointed just beyond the beagles, where I saw Poppa on the ground.

"There, Izzy, let's go!" he shouted.

Izzy had never galloped. Doctor Russ didn't ask, but still we charged onto the field. Izzy grabbed even more mane, and we raced to Poppa.

I called across the field to all who could hear. "I'm coming! Macadoo, the Belgian, is coming!"

The mares and geldings of the hunt club whinnied back, and all the horses and dogs moved out of my path.

Poppa held a bandage to his head, and his hunting jacket lay draped over his leg. He waved when he saw us. "Finally! Izzy, you've come! I wanted to see you, to tell you."

"Judge, you're going to be fine," said Doctor Russ. "You need to get to a doctor about that leg. It may take a while, but you'll be fine."

Poppa's faced paled, and he held his leg tighter. Izzy jumped down, ran the stirrups up the saddle, and slipped the reins beneath the stirrups. By doing this, Izzy was asking me to stand in this place until he came back. He pushed his way through the people crowded around Poppa. "Are you all right?" he asked.

"I think so." Poppa wiped his forehead and nodded. "Job took a long spot over the fence down at the bottom of the hill. Is that right?"

"Poppa, you mean Molly. You rode her today," Izzy corrected his grandfather.

Doctor Russ, who had dismounted the mule, spoke up. "Your Poppa wasn't riding Molly. I was. He took my green horse, Picasso, out today. He's right about the long spot over the fence. Picasso clipped it just enough to throw Judge here off balance and out of the saddle."

"I'm still not sure how I ended up sprawled out in the grass or how my helmet came off. My head hurts." Poppa winced. "My leg, too." He reached in his jacket pocket, pulled out a flask, and took a swig.

Izzy asked him, "Poppa, what are you drinking?"

Poppa held the container out. "Here."

Izzy smelled the bottle, then took a sip. "Cider." He smiled and bent down to kiss his poppa.

We stayed on the field until the ambulance took Poppa away; then we walked home through the forest. Everything about our lives changed that day.

CHAPTER TWENTY-THREE

Mira Stella

Poppa went to the hospital, and we went home to Cedarmont without him. When Izzy and I trotted back out of the woods, Job was standing guard at the gate, awaiting us, like he said he would be. Doctor Russ turned Molly out with Job and me. Izzy didn't correct him and I was glad. I didn't chase the white ducks or charge the sparrows that day. We all wanted to be together to await Poppa's return.

Molly blamed herself, but how could she have changed Poppa's decision about riding the young, green horse? "You know Poppa," Job consoled her. "Stubborn as you."

Izzy stayed out in the paddock with us well past nightfall. Even when Doctor Russ came out to get him, Izzy wouldn't leave. A trace of moon peeked in and out of the clouds and made only a dim light. With no wishing stars in sight, I wished anyway that Poppa would be well and hurry home.

Poppa didn't come back to Cedarmont. Izzy went to stay with Doctor Russ, but still came to tend to us every day. During the daytime and nighttime, Izzy left the gate between our two fields open so Molly, Job, and I could graze freely together.

One evening some weeks later when the nights turned cold, Izzy visited for a long while with us in the pasture. Like always, he scrambled atop my back. He took a flashlight from his pocket and read from his notebook. This time he had written about Poppa, not birds or weather or insects:

"Poppa sat up today and ate oatmeal, toast, and black coffee. He tried to read the paper. I read it to him, then Poppa fell asleep. His doctor says to keep the room dark. I don't know when he can come home or when I can come home either. I'm staying with Doctor Russ till Poppa gets better."

"I like Doctor Russ all right," Izzy said later that night. "Even though I can take care of myself. I'll be fourteen soon. I could take care of Cedarmont for

Poppa, too, but it's Doctor Russ who's making decisions for Poppa."

Izzy closed up his notebook and stretched out on his back. I stopped grazing to give him a steady place to recline and stargaze.

"Let's see if we can find Cetus, the whale. Do you know why I love Cetus, Mac?" Izzy asked.

I flicked my tail to keep him talking.

"A special star lives in Cetus. One called Mira Stella—the wonderful star. Macadoo, how do I tell you about Mira? Mira isn't like all of these other stars. Mira is different; Mira goes away, then comes back."

I nickered, but not so loud as to awaken Job.

Izzy rested his head on his arms. "Almost anytime, I could find the North Star, Polaris. It's always there, every night." Izzy sat up. He wrapped his arms around my neck. "But Mira shines brilliantly for weeks, then fades away to nothing, and to us, it looks like the star's gone completely out. Sometimes, it even seems like Mira may never come back. If you find Cetus—the whale—you can see Mira there, shining brightly, and if not, that's where she'll be when she comes back. She's always there, whether we can see her or not. Poppa told me that story when I first came here. He was trying to make me feel better about Mom; only she will never come back."

Izzy pointed to all the pictures in the sky that he had taught me: Pegasus, Bear, Dipper, and the Great Dog. "Do you remember them, Mac? Never forget, okay?" he said.

I searched the valley sky for the wonderful star, Mira. Each looked wonderful to me. I blew out a long breath and ate some fescue.

In our silence, we watched the stars and planets rise and rest over Shenandoah, the Valley of the Stars. Izzy pulled his knees up into a ball and sighed. "I'm sorry, Mac."

The next day, when Izzy came to feed us, I knew from his tear-streaked face that the story of Mira Stella had been his way of saying good-bye. It was time for me to go.

Izzy placed my leather halter around me. "You should have something of your own to take with you," Izzy said. "This one with your name. Macadoo."

Izzy hooked the lead to my halter and led me out of the barn. A stranger was waiting there with a trailer that was not ours. Doctor Russ walked with us.

"Izzy," the vet said. "I wish I'd found a better solution for Mac. I thought Tamworth Springs might take all three. Molly is a seasoned hunter so their hunt club wants her, and no horse knows Saddle Mountain like Job does, so the riding school could use him to take kids out on trails. But Tamworth Springs said they can't take on a Belgian right now. Mac doesn't know how to jump and Belgians can be harder to keep than other breeds. I tried, son, but your granddad's bills are mounting up and I'm sure Mac will find a good home."

Izzy tightened his grip on my lead rope. "Doctor Russ, can't you take Mac? He's as good a horse as Molly and Job. Poppa always says so."

"No, I don't have the time to keep any horses of my own these days. I know it doesn't seem fair, but I tried. This is a tough time for all horses."

Izzy started to cry. "Please, there must be someone else who needs him."

"I'm sorry. Your Poppa didn't take this decision well either, but neither time nor money is on his side. There's an auction tomorrow in Lynchville. Mac will find a good buyer there."

Now I could not breathe. A sharp pain clamped my gut. I thought if I could roll on the ground I might feel better. If I could just walk in the field with Izzy, everything would be better. I danced around too much to load, and Doctor Russ tried to take me from my boy.

"Best if I do this," the vet said. "He's having a hard time."

Izzy held me tight. "Mac'd do anything for me. I'll walk him up; he's a good horse." Izzy sobbed into my neck; I nickered into his.

Izzy hopped into the trailer first. He clucked and I

did the thing I loved and hated to do. I loved to please Izzy, and I hated to go away. I jumped right up into the dark place.

Izzy touched my marked ear. "Be a good boy and remember." Izzy wiped his eyes on his sleeve, then buried his face in my shoulder. "Mira Stella, right, boy?"

I nuzzled my boy's hair.

The driver grew impatient for Izzy to say good-bye. "This horse is young; he'll be fine. Come on, now."

Izzy kissed me good-bye.

The truck started up; its engine knocked loud in my ears. As the trailer pulled out of the drive, through the window I heard Izzy shouting after me, "Don't forget me, Mac. Don't forget!"

CHAPTER TWENTY-FOUR

The Virginia Auction

When the trailer opened I was back at auction. The driver signed a paper; he handed my lead to a sun-leathered man, taller than Poppa and even taller than John Macadoo.

"Oh, the boys will like the size of you," he said. "Must be more than seventeen hands, probably close to two thousand pounds. The boys will like to get ahold of you, all right."

The Virginia auction house was smaller than the one I had survived in Alberta. In the queue behind the auction were two miniature donkeys chained to a post, pigs galore rooting all around, and six nanny goats bleating and racing around a small pen. Dozens of Black Angus awaited their fates, too.

A hollow dairy cow rested on the other side of the fence, away from the unwanted menagerie. Just past the cow, a frail Thoroughbred filly stood alone. The filly was all but a ghost.

The round man guarding the pens said, "This one sealed her fate first time out."

"Sam says she's a great-granddaughter of Secretariat," another, younger, one said. "Seems a waste."

The man in charge was not impressed. "Aw, heck, Curtis. This filly hardly matters. What matters is, can they run? Straight outta the gate, this little spitfire threw her jockey, then jumped the track. It's a wonder they didn't put her down then and there. I reckon her owner was trying to get away from taking care of business on-site, so here she is."

"Look at her; she's gorgeous," said the man called Curtis. "If I had money in my pocket, I'd buy her. Shoot, have a descendant of Secretariat? I'd love that."

"All you got is an empty pocket. Anyway, this filly's so bad off she might not even make it to market. I'm afraid nothing could help her today."

To keep the auction moving quickly, the filly and I were bundled together. At this auction, there were no children, no fancy ladies, and no cowboys with shiny belt buckles. No one strolled by our pen.

The older worker shoved me, then the filly, toward the chute. He held a prod to my hind, but I tried to keep peace between us. Knowing that I was still a fine Belgian, a purebred from Alberta, I walked into the auction house freely. Wherever I might go, I would bring with me the scar on my ear, the leather halter bearing my name, and my willingness to serve—all I had to remind me who I was.

At that moment, the filly needed me most. I could do little but befriend and comfort her. Her head drooped, and her shoulders sagged. She looked defeated.

"What's your name?" She didn't answer until the third time I asked.

"I don't have a real name. I have a Jockey Club name, a family name, but that's not me. I'm not a race-horse; not anymore."

"Why did you throw your jockey?"

"I didn't throw him. I started fierce, on the gun, just as I had been trained to do. He steered me into a crowd on the rail, and I stumbled. He rolled over my head."

"Why did you jump the track?"

Her eyes brightened, and she whickered recalling it. "Because I love to jump. That's all."

The workers moved us closer to the auction floor.

The filly pinned her ears at them and flared her eyes white.

"Listen," I told her. "This will be over soon; then we'll know what's next for us. When we're inside, there will be bright lights and loud noises. Men yelling terrible things. Close your mind to all of it. Think of someone you love."

"I don't love anyone," she said.

"Think of something you love, then. Jumping! Nothing else."

When the door opened to the sale going on inside, I saw the auctioneer sitting up high in a box. Smiling and talking too fast, he set his glasses on top of his head. He greeted each bidder by his first name.

The filly hadn't time to ask me any questions. They led us into the auction house; the steel door slammed behind us. Inside, just five bidders sat waiting. I arched my neck, the way Molly had in her lessons with Poppa, the way my father did on the hill in Alberta. I walked over to the auctioneer to get a look and a sniff and to draw attention away from the underweight filly and onto me.

"Get on out front!" the workingman shouted, and stung me with the prod. The filly kept her head up and her gaze on me.

The auctioneer held his arm out toward us with a flourish; then to the men in the stands, he said, "Lot one-twenty-seven. Got a nice Belgian, boys; get a good look. He's right friendly and healthy, too. Healthiest horse we got here today. Every bit of nineteen hundred pounds, maybe two gee. The filly here's a great-granddaughter of Secretariat, one of the greatest Thoroughbred horses in modern history. She's Virginia-born, gentlemen. The Belgian's cleft in the ear, as you can see, but he'll make a real nice pet."

The kill buyers laughed. "Pet food, ya mean, Jimmy! But you didn't hear me say that."

"Now, boys, the Belgian belonged to Judge Harry Isler out in Buena Vista. Comes to you from just down the road. Been well cared for, as you can see. A companion to man and child alike. How about nine hundred? Come on, boys; don't let him go to Mexico. No, no, no, not to Mexico. Not Canada either. Help me out; keep this purebred draft and this grand filly out of the slaughterhouses."

The bidders stared down at their boots.

The auctioneer talked fast and faster. "Take a good look, now, boys! Nine hundred; nine hundred. Eight fifty? Boys, I'm old; I'm tired. Don't make me work this hard. I'll keep you here all night—eight forty-five, eight forty, eight thirty-five. See what I mean? All right, eight hundred. Seven hundred; six fifty. What's it gonna take, fine Belgian like this? Six hundred. Six hundred. Five hundred. Four hundred. Three?"

One of the bidders nodded.

"At last, and I thank you. Three hundred, and I don't want to know where they're going to go. Is that it? Are we all through and all done? Allen, put your hand down unless you're offering three fifty."

The far door opened and I whinnied to see who had come.

"Stop!"

A lady walked in from the back—a lady with a floppy straw hat, a lady like Janey only not Janey.

Standing in the midst of the farmers, the new lady held up her hat and yelled to the auctioneer, "Five hundred, Jimmy, and let's be done. I want this Belgian for my therapeutic riding school. A friend called me and told me to run up here and save him from these fools, and here I am. Five hundred; now, slam that hammer down."

The auctioneer banged down his hammer. "Five hundred to Isbell Maiden. Isbell, you are an angel. I dreamed of you last night. May I take you to dinner?"

The bidding men howled like hunting dogs.

Before the filly or I could relax, the lady who had stopped the auction delivered bad news. "I can't take the filly, though. I'm afraid I'll have to let her go with one of you scoundrels," she said.

The young man who had worked our pen spoke up.

"Mrs. Maiden? Remember me? Curtis! I used to ride with you at the Maury River Stables when I was a kid."

"Curtis, I could never forget you. You were a fidgety mess but as sweet as you could be. And you still have all those freckles."

He laughed and moved closer to us. "Could I ask you a favor? Please, don't give her to those buyers. I'll treat her well; you know I will." Curtis stroked the filly's neck. "We have a barn and plenty of room. Could I take her?"

The filly whickered and Mrs. Maiden grinned. "That's the easiest favor I've ever been asked to do. She's yours, Curtis."

"Woo-hoo!" He threw his arms around Mrs. Maiden and lifted her up off the ground, so high that the lady lost her hat. "Oh, gosh, sorry, Mrs. Maiden," he said, and set her down.

The auctioneer interrupted them. "Are you two about done with the side business? I sure don't mean to interrupt this very important transaction. I've got fifty head of cattle, six goats, and twenty pigs to get through today. Isbell, do you mind?"

When Mrs. Maiden came with a lead rope, my lip was still shaking. She fluffed up my forelock. "Hi, Macadoo. I went to school with Judge Isler's daughter, Charlotte, so he called me this morning. I wish he had thought of me first, but it doesn't matter now. He wondered if I might need a new therapeutic riding horse, which I do! Judge tells me you're as reliable as those old mules he's been riding around the county for decades."

Izzy and Poppa had saved me. And, in a way, Charlotte had, too.

"He said his grandson was inconsolable when you left and I do need another horse for my therapeutic program. I'll put you to work as a school horse and in the vaulting program, too. Come on, let's get you home."

The worker opened the door and led me back to the pen. The Thoroughbred filly passed by me with her head up. We walked just close enough to say good-bye and then each walked on to our new homes.

CHAPTER TWENTY-FIVE

The Maury River Stables

Mrs. Maiden loaded me in the trailer and we started on the road to her riding school, the Maury River Stables. She left the window open so I could breathe in the cool October mountain air. Mrs. Maiden drove carefully—I didn't slip or slide once—and I reached her barn without one new mark on my hind or barrel, though I had plenty from the auction house.

The trailer pulled up to a common-looking barn at the foot of Saddle Mountain, whose two summits come together to resemble Izzy's English saddle. I blew a long breath out over the gravel drive. I could see the blue mountains in every direction, but this place was not my home. My home, Cedarmont, was just on the other side.

Mrs. Maiden turned me out in a small pen beside the barn with a small run-in and two old cedars whose trunks had grown together into one. I trotted back and forth at the gate, looking for a way out.

The woman placed three flakes of hay in the run-in. "That's right, boy, relax. Take it all in. Don't worry. We're going to treat you right," Mrs. Maiden promised.

I stood away, just watching her that first day. At suppertime, she called me to her.

"Macadoo! You might as well go on and come here to me." Her voice was not the glorious sound of my boy Izzy's, but it was kindly all the same.

I hid behind the cedar's wide trunk.

"You're a draft horse. That tree doesn't even hide your backside. You know that? I can see almost all of you." Mrs. Maiden held the water hose in her hand in a long arc; its spray fell just shy of me.

When she turned the hose toward me again, I walked to the middle of the field. She bent to clean out the old, empty tub. She leaned far into the tub, pulling hay and muck from its bottom. Water drained out and rolled across the bare ground to my feet. I followed the water trail to Mrs. Maiden and rumbled into her ear.

"Oh! Well, hello. You startled me." She stood up.

I could have run, but the sound of water made me stay. I was thirsty.

"Hey there, boy, come here." Mrs. Maiden grabbed for my halter.

I took a step back.

"Shhh . . . hold on, hold on." She aimed the hose at one of the swollen cuts on my leg. "How about that? Is that better?"

I nickered; the cold water felt good.

Mrs. Maiden brought me into the barn and carefully cleaned the marks from the prod at the auction. "I hadn't realized they hurt you. I'll be right back."

She returned with liniment and apples and giggling girls. Little ones, big ones, and even grown ones circled me, all holding brushes, sponges, and treats. They liked my halter, and they liked my name.

"Macadoo!"

"Oh, somebody loved you! Look at this; he's got a leather halter with a nameplate. I want one!"

"Macadoo! Fan-cee!"

While tiny hands braided my mane and tail, Mrs. Maiden told the girls, "Judge Isler, from other side the county, got Macadoo as a colt for his grandson four years ago. The judge had a riding accident in September. Broke his leg in three places and suffered a pretty bad concussion. Now he and his grandson have moved to a smaller place in the city."

"Didn't they want Macadoo anymore, Mrs. Maiden?" one of the young girls asked.

"Oh, I know they wanted him, but horses and a boy are a lot to take care of for someone of any age. I've heard his medical bills are pretty high. Judge Isler just couldn't do it anymore, and now we have this nice horse. How about if we give Mac a try as a lesson horse. Would you ladies like that?"

"He's perfect!" said the girl stretching up on her toes to reach my forelock.

"He's so big!" said the child at my chest. "I don't know if I want to ride him till I'm older."

"Hey, what happened to his ear?" chimed in the little girl standing on a mounting block, braiding my mane.

"Well, he's very quiet and standing nicely for you girls," said Mrs. Maiden. "I like that. What do you think, Naomi?"

I noticed another girl off to the side, squatting on top of a crate, watching me. Her eyes were hidden, covered by her own curly forelock, but she was watching me.

"He's too big," she said.

Mrs. Maiden answered patiently. "Yes, he is big. He's a Belgian draft. He's supposed to be big. He's probably close to eighteen hands. I think he's five years old, so I don't expect he'll grow too much bigger. He's very gentle. Come see for yourself."

"No, I'm stayin' right here," Naomi said as she moved farther from me.

"Good gracious, Naomi. Go get an apple from the tack room. Let me show you that it's all right to be near Mac." Mrs. Maiden waved her over.

Naomi shook her head.

The other girls giggled.

"Shut up! I'm not scared. I'm just not coming over there, because I don't want to."

Mrs. Maiden walked to Naomi and held her hand out. "Come with me. I'll stand with you while you meet Mac."

The girl came and stood directly behind me, in the one spot where I could see nothing. Still, I didn't mind her being there. Another horse might have minded a great deal and might well have flicked his tail or even kicked, but I had learned patience from the mules.

"You never stand directly behind a horse. You might get kicked. Now, calm down and come here." Mrs. Maiden tried again. "Notice how wide his back is? And look at the muscles he has here." Mrs. Maiden stroked my shoulders and chest. "Belgians are bred to pull heavy loads and to carry a lot of weight comfortably. If you look at Saddle Mountain, in fact, you can tell that the trees are not all that old. Do you know why?"

The girls all shrugged.

"Because horses like Mac here logged that mountain—and mountains all over the country—years ago. Belgians are bred for two things: a good disposition and a strong build."

I reached my neck around as far back as I could to see Naomi. She smelled of apple, so I reached my lips out, too.

"Ahhh!" She screamed and pulled away. "Is he going to eat me?"

"Naomi, you're a trip." Mrs. Maiden laughed. "Horses eat apples, not people. You know that. Come back here."

A car horn honked twice. "That's my foster mom. I gotta go now," Naomi said, and ran from the barn.

The other girls kept misting my legs with fly spray and buffing my coat with a dandy brush. They fed me carrots and peppermints and wondered if they could ride me.

From the paddock, I could see that the drive beside the barn ran out to the road that led back to Cedarmont. I could have run across the Maury River, up Saddle Mountain, and all the way to Cedarmont, but even I knew my old life with Izzy was gone.

✴ CHAPTER TWENTY-SIX ✴

Who Am I Now?

On my first day in the gelding field at the Maury River Stables, the October sun burned the morning fog away, and I could see my splendid mountains in every direction. Just beyond the back fence line, the Maury River ran shallow between banks of sycamore, closer to me than it was at Cedarmont.

Here I lived in a field with Charlie, Cowboy, and Jake, who were boarded horses, and Dante and an overweight Shetland pony named Napoleon, who were lesson horses owned by Mrs. Maiden. I towered over all of them.

The black Thoroughbred gelding, Dante, ruled our field, and he seemed unimpressed that I outweighed him by almost one thousand pounds and that my shadow fell longer than his, too. I could have taken charge of the geldings anytime, but I didn't want to. I wanted Cedarmont and Izzy.

Poppa had once described the Belgian breed as half work and half love. Mrs. Maiden gave me a job. I worked without complaint for the woman who saved me from the auction and for the children in her care, teaching the older ones and their mothers to ride, and standing still while Mrs. Maiden used me to teach everyone all about chestnuts, frogs, docks, and horse feathers.

There was a different child to meet every day, it seemed. Their names and faces all blended together. I did my best to learn this new way of being a horse. Mrs. Maiden was always kind and always on time with grain and hay and turnout. But it wasn't the same.

While Cedarmont was a family estate where Judge Isler kept a riding ring and trails, just for pleasure, the Maury River Stables was a business. Poppa had bought me to help restore Izzy's spirit. But Mrs. Maiden had bid on me, at the auction, for a different purpose: to work in her school with many different children.

Half love. Half work. Yet one half was still missing. Girls and boys here came and went as quickly as the clouds moved across the valley.

As a colt, I had learned to live with the absence

of part of my ear, and I had learned to live without Mamere, but how could I live without Izzy?

All through the autumn, I watched for Izzy every day, sure he would return for me as soon as he and Poppa could. At the sound of a car door slamming, I would canter to the gate and wait to hear Izzy call, "Macadoo! It's me!"

But car doors opened and closed all the time without bringing Izzy.

The stars helped me remember Izzy though. At the end of each day's work, the night sky was my solace. I tried to find Bear, Dipper, and Pegasus. When I looked for Polaris and Cetus, I knew Izzy was somewhere watching them, too.

Each night I chose one light in the sky to focus on; I sometimes selected the star shining brightest in the sky and other nights I picked the one hanging nearest the moon. In the light and dark of that infinite space, I remembered Izzy.

But a loving memory is not the same as love.

One night a dense, low sky had settled over the Maury River Stables, and I couldn't see the stars that helped me remember my boy.

The tangles awoke in me again. Up and down the hill I paced, searching for a window through the fog — a moon ring, or a patch of bright stars — but I could only see my own feet and not much more. I thought if I could just roll on the ground to make the pain go away, then I might feel better in the morning.

I jumped up when I heard Gwen, a Hanoverian mare, trot up on the other side of the fence line. She walked beside me in the mare field, on her side of our shared fence. She asked, "Have you lost your way?"

I could hear but could not see her. "Lost?"

She nickered. "You've worn down a hard path over there. Are you in distress?"

"Go away." I pinned my ears. "I don't feel good. I want to be alone."

The warmblood nickered softly to me. "Sweetest," Gwen said, and I thought of Mamere. No one else had ever called me "sweetest." "Why don't I stay with you awhile?"

I pushed my ears down, flat against my head, and squealed at her.

"All right, sweet Mac. I will go," Gwen said.

But she did not leave; she grazed alone, in the mare field next to me. I heard her pulling at the grass, though the fog engulfed all but her legs.

She will have to wait all night, I thought, *if she is waiting for me.*

Along the fence post, I feigned grazing but could not eat. The mare across the fence from me had three white socks, just like Mamere.

I rumbled to Gwen.

The blood bay reached her head across the fence. She nuzzled me.

"I saw your mules at Tamworth Springs when I hunted there last week," she said. "They send their love and their breath."

"Molly and Job?" I whinnied to know more.

"Oh, I've known them for years. These days, we speak of you quite a bit — that is, until we hear *tallyho.* Then, we don't speak at all; we race behind the hounds. Job told me how you like to race." This time, Gwen leaned across the fence and nipped at me. "Is that true?"

I hung my head. I had not raced anyone, or anywhere, since Cedarmont.

"What is it you want, Mac?" Gwen asked.

Her question startled me, but I spoke the truth, because Mamere raised me so. "What I want is to be with all of my family: Mamere and Molly and Job and Poppa and Izzy."

"I see." Gwen turned to leave. The three white socks started down the hill.

"Wait, please. So, you know my mules?"

"Yes, but they are not here," she said.

I shoved my shoulder into the fence; it shook down the line. "They would want you to help me!"

Gwen spun around to face me. "I didn't know your dam, but I know the mules and I imagine they would be saddened to see that you still resist your nature, your true purpose. Count yourself lucky. You have been spared not once, but twice."

The fog started its drift into the valley.

"Gwen?" I asked for her breath. "Who am I without my family? What do I do now without them?"

She sent her breath to me. "Can't you see? You're well loved here. By me, Mrs. Maiden, and all the students. Who are you? I'll tell you. You are a fine Belgian. What do you do now? You love and you work, Mac. And when you have a favorite child again and when that next child leaves, guess what you do then. You love and you work. That is all you need to do, for that is who you are."

I asked Gwen one more question. "What else did Molly and Job say?"

Gwen nickered. "Molly asked if you had tried to jump out of the field yet. Job told me that if you got too bothersome, I should tell you to go away."

"Oh. Is that all?"

The mare nodded toward the sky. "Have you ever heard of a star called Mira?"

"Yes!" My stomach started to rumble. Walking and talking with Gwen had helped me feel better.

"Job muttered something about Mira. He asked me to remind you to remember Izzy's story."

I nickered. "Job was in the field with Izzy and me that night, but I didn't know he was listening, too!"

Gwen and I grazed next to each other, with only a fence line between us, for many nights after. I stayed awake and walking, wondering if each star I could not see might be the wonderful star that would bring Izzy back to me. Until our reunion, I would fulfill my promise to serve at the Maury River Stables.

CHAPTER TWENTY-SEVEN

Hop Aboard

I still watched for Izzy every day, but I slowly eased into my work. I learned the sights and sounds and smells of Mrs. Maiden's riding school and assisted children with all sorts of riding—beginner lessons on the flat, some jumping, trails, and the beginnings of what Mrs. Maiden called dressage.

And, Mrs. Maiden evaluated me for use with her vaulting team—first by longeing me, just as Poppa had done. Then she longed me at the walk in a circle with Ashley, an older, more advanced student who was the captain of the vaulting team.

Then Ashley rode without a saddle. Mrs. Maiden instructed her to swing around and ride facing backward. Then Ashley stretched out along my back, in just the same way Izzy had liked to watch birds and stars, though I had always made sure to stand still for Izzy.

Next, after mounting and sitting astride for four beats, Ashley moved from the basic seat into flag by pushing herself up on all fours, then stretching her right leg and left arm straight out in opposite directions. The handles of the surcingle, the point of her left knee, and the curve of my back supported her. From there she'd do a mill: a series of leg passes. Starting from a basic seat she'd swing her straight legs and pointed toes up over my neck and then over my croup, my croup and then my neck again, traveling "around the world," while I traveled around and around Mrs. Maiden in the middle.

"He's doing great, isn't he? Oh, I love him. There's so much room to move around on Mac. He doesn't seem to mind whatever I do," said Ashley.

"So far, so good," Mrs. Maiden agreed. "Let's throw something harder at him. You ready?"

"Ready!" said Ashley.

Mrs. Maiden asked me to trot, and Ashley returned to sitting face forward.

When Mrs. Maiden asked me to canter, I obeyed.

Then Ashley moved to kneeling, then standing.

I could feel the smile on Ashley's face and see it on Mrs. Maiden's.

I proved that I was willing to carry two then three riders at once on my back, each of them standing and turning and lifting one another at the walk, trot, or canter. I caught glimpses of arms and legs turning and twirling behind me—on me—while Mrs. Maiden kept me moving at a steady pace.

Poppa would put a stop to this, I thought. *Poppa would never go for all this standing and twirling on a horse. But Izzy would love to know about a kind of riding made up of tricks and flips.*

And I liked it, too.

I worked hard and tried to become a good vaulting horse, ever-solid and ever-present to the shifting weight and balance of my students. In vaulting, the aids came from Mrs. Maiden in the center of the circle, but I could never ever, even for a moment lose touch with my riders. Listening to many people, I worked doubly hard, and I enjoyed it.

Naomi, the girl who had been so afraid of me at first, grew ever more confident and comfortable around the barn. Lately, I had even noticed her imitating Ashley on the vaulting barrel beside the ring.

The barrel helped students find balance and gain confidence in their vaulting skills by being able to practice tricks over and over on the ground before trying something new on me.

One spring morning, Naomi brought me in from the field and hitched me to the grooming post in the barn. She wasn't wearing paddock boots or jodhpurs, so I guessed that she wanted to learn to vault.

She hadn't come near me since my first day at the Maury River Stables, when she was so scared. This time she bravely started to groom me. She circled the currycomb around the mud caked on my legs and stomach. Her heart, next to my cheek, beat quickly, which I knew for Izzy meant "fear," so I imagined myself a smaller horse.

Mrs. Maiden brought over a mounting block. "Here, hop aboard. You've brushed the bottom half, but we've got to get the dirt off the rest of him. Now, really brush him good up there. Otherwise, all that dirt will irritate his back once he's tacked up." Mrs. Maiden patted my shoulder.

Naomi brushed me clean, then Mrs. Maiden placed a large blanket and a thick pad over my back.

"Doesn't that look comfortable? Now we'll add the surcingle," Mrs. Maiden said. She situated a wide leather girth made with sturdy handles on top.

As we walked from the barn to the riding ring, Naomi wanted to know all about me from Mrs. Maiden.

"When I walked into the field, all of the other geldings were running and racing, but Mac stood alone. He came right up to me like he wanted leave the field and ride, not play. Is he a sad horse?"

"Did you know I rescued this horse from an auction?" Mrs. Maiden said.

"Do you think maybe he feels like nobody wants him?"

Mrs. Maiden stopped and looked at me. "He might.

Maybe a little bit. You know, this is at least Mac's fourth home in just a few years. He's survived so much. I don't know if he's sad, but I imagine he's a little unsure. What he needs is stability. When he figures out that's what he has here, he'll come around."

The child tickled me under my chin. "Smile!" Naomi told me.

Inside the ring, before she mounted, Naomi tightened the surcingle's buckle with Mrs. Maiden's help.

"I know one thing for sure. Every horse here is wanted and loved. Now, get your shoes off and hop aboard," Mrs. Maiden said.

"How old is Mac in people years?" Naomi asked.

Mrs. Maiden gave Naomi a leg up and hooked the longe line to my halter. "Well, every horse year is equal to three human years. I don't have his papers so I can't tell you for sure, but I think he's about five. Maybe four. So, Mac is the people equivalent of somewhere between twelve and fifteen."

"I'm twelve!" the girl said. "Where I live now is my fourth home, too. Some families have been nice to me; some haven't. Where I live now, my foster mom loves me, so don't worry — everything will turn out all right for you, too, Mac.

"I really get to ride in my socks?" Naomi asked.

"Yes. Now, relax and breathe. Seated like that, facing forward and sitting up with both hands on the surcingle bars, is your basic seat in vaulting. It's called astride. Everything you learn will build from here. Eyes forward; ears on me. Raise your arms up alongside your ears. Palms out. I'll control Mac."

Like always in vaulting, Mrs. Maiden and I formed the course ourselves by creating a small working circle inside the big riding ring. Mrs. Maiden stood in the center, using a whip and a longe line to direct the pace at which I traced the circle. I only stopped moving at Mrs. Maiden's request or if my rider lost balance, and even then, sometimes, Mrs. Maiden would crack the whip near my hindquarters to remind me to keep going.

Naomi started out at the walk. She lifted her arms straight out from her shoulders.

"Are those your ears?" Mrs. Maiden asked.

The girl giggled.

Mrs. Maiden giggled, too. "Now, try to relax and feel Mac's walk."

Over the weeks, during our lessons, I kept one ear always on Mrs. Maiden and one ear always on Naomi, who took to vaulting like the Canada geese had taken to chasing me through my old paddock.

If Naomi turned to watch Mrs. Maiden explain something new, Mrs. Maiden corrected her. "Why are you looking at me? Listen and look ahead, always ahead. And point those toes; pretend like you're a ballerina up there, Naomi."

Week after week, we improved. As the days turned dark and short, my winter coat grew as long and thick as ever, and Naomi's vaulting lessons moved indoors. She wore wool gloves, a down coat, and a grin on her face that I could feel even in the touch of her hands.

Naomi learned to move fluidly with all of her body, using all of mine for support. Her hands strong on the surcingle and her feet pressed into my dock made a push-up, a nice warm-up position to remind Naomi that she would need all her length and her strength. One leg extended long along my crest, a bent knee resting on my croup, and arms reaching head to tail were her favorite position — an advanced move called special K.

For an hour each week, Naomi learned and practiced her compulsory moves, a basic set of positions that every vaulter must master, link together, and perform in order.

Scissors was the hardest for me and for the rider. In this trick, Naomi would press her weight into the surcingle handles, then swing herself into the air, crisscross her legs, and twist her body to land facing my tail. It took lots of hard landings for Naomi to develop enough strength to make the move look graceful and to soften her landings on my back.

By springtime, Naomi moved from trick to trick smoothly and with ease. Naomi and I had shed our coats — much of mine was shed on her and my other students as they groomed me — and she was vaulting all her movements at a trot, and trying some at the canter. Now Naomi wore her own special shoes with grips on the soles, made just for vaulting—a gift from her foster mother.

At last, Mrs. Maiden told her, "You're ready to stand."

During our lesson one morning, Naomi's foster mother came out especially to watch us. Like always, Naomi curried and brushed me before our lesson. I was sorry that I had gotten so dirty on a day when we had an audience to impress, but the girl didn't seem to mind. She was thinking about our routine.

"I warmed up on the barrel, Macadoo. I'm ready. Are you?" she asked me.

I am ready. I told her with my stillness. *I am ready.*

An early sun and daylight moon framed the riding ring, giving Saddle Mountain clarity and brilliance. The mountain gave me confidence. I relied on Saddle Mountain to be there for me every day; it told me I was home. Naomi could rely on me that way. I imagined myself wide and broad, gentle and strong like a mountain in this child's service.

Mrs. Maiden clipped the longe line to me, and with a flick of the whip in the air, I started to trot. Naomi ran along beside me, grabbed hold of the surcingle, and mounted on her own. She moved silently from basic seat to flag to mill. She sat for four beats, then swung up into scissors and landed backward so softly that I didn't wobble or jerk my head at all. The scissors return done in reverse brought her back to sitting astride. From there, she hopped up onto her shins, then to her feet, and then Naomi pressed up to standing. She raised her arms high and stood tall on my back.

For ten strides, she balanced on my back, high up off the ground while I trotted a circle. She drew upon all of the strength in her legs and her torso and her back. With her back straight and her chin up and a slight bend in her knees, she shone.

"Ready to show off your special dismount?" Mrs. Maiden asked her.

She prepared for the last move, a flank: starting with a handstand into side seat, with both legs on the inside.

From side seat, Naomi returned to sitting astride, leaned backward, lifted her legs, and somersaulted off of my back. She landed firmly, confidently, on her feet. I halted beside her and nickered.

Naomi wasn't afraid of me anymore. She had used my size and my power to help her become a star. She even became the captain of the vaulting team after Ashley started leasing Dante. And, when the day came that she left the Maury River Stables, finally to return to her first home, she was a stronger girl.

"Thank you," she whispered to me that day. "I never thought I could ride a horse without being afraid, but I can. I love you, Mac."

My strength had helped Naomi find hers.

★ CHAPTER TWENTY-EIGHT ★

Another New Job

I wouldn't say I forgot Izzy, not at all. I was surrounded by nature and creatures that Izzy loved and that he had taught me to love, too. In daytime, I noticed birds that Izzy had first shown me—like the tiny phoebe, who called out her name, "Phee-bee! Phee-bee!" At nighttime, surrounded by moon and sky and stars, I could always make out Pegasus. And I saw that Izzy was right: Mira Stella left the night sky for a very long time. I searched the sky for her every night until the sun rose. And then I went to work again.

I started training for a new job at the Maury River Stables, too. Mrs. Maiden told me that I could work in the therapeutic riding school.

"I had to test you a bit first," Mrs. Maiden said. "In the therapeutic program, your special job will be to accept each student for who they are and what they present to the lesson. You'll learn to sense even the smallest hopes that each student brings to our barn and learn how to make those hopes grow even brighter."

My friend Gwen also worked in the therapeutic school.

"Mrs. Maiden says you change people's lives in the therapeutic school. Is that true?" I asked Gwen one day at our regular meeting place, the high corner where the mare and gelding fields joined.

She flicked me with her tail. "The therapeutic school isn't that different from the lessons you teach now. Sometimes, we even teach vaulting in the therapeutic program. We always attend to whoever sits in the saddle, whatever their needs are. Besides, all horses change lives, Macadoo."

"By working hard?"

"Partly."

"How else?"

The Hanoverian reached out to me. "Leave yesterday behind. Today you are here, Macadoo. Let today be your joy and you will bring joy to all those you serve."

Mrs. Maiden's barn manager, a gentle man named Stu, prepared me for the therapeutic school. He showed me shiny objects; he rolled twine across my shoulders and withers — all to teach me still and quiet manners.

Stu took me on solitary rides around Saddle Mountain to get me used to the unpredictable world around me, but I already knew all the sights and sounds of the mountains. Stu and Mrs. Maiden didn't understand: I had grown up with the splendid mountains. With Izzy. And Poppa, Molly, and Job. My training for the therapeutic school had started all the way back at Cedarmont.

The mountain was like a good and true friend, and Stu found that I could not be spooked on or off the old logging trails. Those roads, cleared long ago by drafts like me, made for an easy path, and nothing scared me. I walked right up to the wild turkey; I trotted over the fallen pines. The Maury River refreshed me on this side of the mountain, too. Off trail, I knew how to step down and up the steep rocks. I never bolted once.

I proved to be a steady and sure worker. In the springtime, Stu told Mrs. Maiden, "If I didn't know he was a hundred percent Belgian, I'd swear to you he had some mule in him. He's ready."

On my first day working in the therapeutic school, Mrs. Maiden strode into our field with my halter slung over her shoulder. "Mac, come on."

I walked over, ready to work.

"I believe you're finally getting used to me. It's

about time." Mrs. Maiden reached up and placed my halter over my ears and buckled it around my cheek. She tacked me up for my first student and Stu led me to the ring, where a child waited at the chair ramp.

As a colt, when I was so scared to leave Mamere, the sound of one boy's voice had given me hope. At the Maury River Stables, there were nice ladies, like Mrs. Maiden, and nice men, like Stu, and so many girls, but I had about lost hope of ever hearing a boy say my name again, when I heard a young boy's voice call me.

"Macadoo! I'm up here!" Eric Sand said. "Look at me!" He sat in his chair on wheels, waiting at the top of the ramp. Izzy might not ever come, but this new boy needed me to be his horse right then, so when he waved at me I nickered back.

"Yeah, Mac!" He pushed his feet down into his chair and leaned back his head. "Ha, ha! He likes me," Eric said to his mother.

Mrs. Maiden stood on the ramp with Eric. Stu guided me even with the ledge and held me straight. I kept still and quiet, just as I had been taught, while Mrs. Maiden eased Eric onto my back and into a specially made saddle for two people.

Eric's mother looked around like something was lost. "My husband, Virgil, should be here any minute to help," she explained. "He'll come; he promised."

"Yeah," said Eric. "My dad's coming."

An old, dented truck turned down the drive and parked on the grass instead of the gravel.

"Sorry I'm late," said Eric's father. He reached out to pat me, his hand rougher than Poppa's, less sure than Stu's, and when I gave him my breath, he pulled back.

Then he breathed a long sigh and looked to Mrs. Maiden. "Should we get started?"

Mrs. Maiden nodded. She told the Sands, "As I understand, you're here because Eric wants to learn to ride. We can do that, but we're going to take it pretty slow. Does that sound fine with you?"

Eric tossed his head back and raised his hand high in the air.

"That means yes," said Virgil Sand.

Mrs. Maiden smiled. "I picked that up. Eric, you look happy sitting up there on Mac. I'm so happy your mom called me. I believe that anyone can learn to ride. Did you ever think you'd get to ride a big horse like this?"

As Mrs. Maiden explained our work, she spoke to Eric directly. "The reason we're going to take our time is because with brain injuries, we want to be sure that we give you and Mac whatever you need together to become a good team. There's a lot to consider— balance, alignment, and how much rest you might need. I want you to be safe and have fun. So, are you ready?"

Eric clapped his hands. "Ready!"

On our first day, Eric sat in that saddle made for two with his father. Mrs. Maiden stood at my head. Stu stood to one side of me, and Eric's mother on the other. Virgil sat behind him with his arms around Eric's waist. I carried them both in the curve of my back. With the strength of my two thousand pounds, I held father and son.

While I walked, I could see the geldings racing one another to the top of the field and back again. I could not run and did not want to, for I was working.

After Eric's first lesson, he waited at the fence line with his father for Stu to turn me out. Stu brought me over to say good-bye first. Eric stayed in his chair, across the fence and near enough to touch my coat. He held his hand out with an apple. I lowered my head and took half of it.

Eric laughed and said, "Again!"

I took the other half and felt one of his fingers in my mouth, too. I didn't bite him, but Eric shrieked.

I tried to nuzzle him an apology through the fence, but heard his father say, "Get away from my boy."

"The horse didn't hurt him, Virgil," said Eric's mother, Amy.

"Yeaaah," Eric called out.

I nickered at the boy. He waved his arm to me.

"That horse is supposed to help Eric, not scare him. That's its job."

His wife said softly, "Did you see Eric laughing? Tell me the last time anything or anybody made Eric laugh." She reached out for her husband's hand. "I'm happy we came here. I love my boy. He's a good boy. I love you. You're a good man. I think this is a good horse. Don't be angry, okay?"

Then Amy Sand gave Virgil a carrot, and he held it out to me. I moved toward him and was careful with my teeth.

Eric swung his head and arm toward me. "Good boy, Mac. Yeah, yeah."

Eric Sand and I worked together on Saturdays, and there were more therapeutic lessons on Tuesdays and Fridays with Joseph and Amelia. The vaulting team practiced with me on Thursdays and Sundays. And I had lessons with the ladies on Wednesdays because very few of the students' mothers could resist the riding ring. Even Mrs. Pickett, who kept a donkey across the road, started taking riding lessons. Though Mira Stella did not return for night after night, every day my students did.

CHAPTER TWENTY-NINE

Claire

The autumn after Naomi left, I met Claire. A child, smaller than any that had ridden me appeared in the gelding field one crisp Saturday morning. Napoleon, the fat Shetland pony, was too busy eating hay to notice. Dante, our black Thoroughbred leader, couldn't waste his time on a child when the other geldings — Charlie, Cowboy, Jake, and a new boarder, George — needed rounding up. So I went to see about her myself. I found her standing by a fence post, talking with sparrows.

Neither Mrs. Maiden nor Stu seemed to have brought the girl to the field. Wearing old, torn overalls and new paddock boots, she stood grinning at me in the tall grass. I remember that her top front teeth were missing then.

"I'm Claire! I'm eight!" she said. "Mrs. Maiden says I get to take my first lesson on Daisy. I would rather ride you. I've read about your breed at the library. You're a Belgian. I love Belgians!"

I had only met one other child, Izzy, who wasn't afraid of me at first because of my size. Claire wanted to feed me by hand. She reached through the fence to a spot beyond my reach. Claire held her palm open and offered me a clump of wet grass.

Carefully, I took it from her — so much sweeter than the overgrazed offerings inside our field.

"You are a gentle giant." She recited this as if it were a fact.

And while I sniffed around for stray clover, Claire told me more about Belgians than I ever expected a child to know.

"A long, long time ago, like, hundreds of years ago, your ancestors were famous. The Great Horse of Flanders, Macadoo, that's you! Knights rode you into battle. Farmers harnessed you to till the soil. That's what the book said, 'till the soil.' I guess Belgians were tractors before there were tractors."

Claire squatted down in the grass beside me. She reached her hand out toward my cannon and fluffed the long hairs growing there. "Nice horse feathers! Your winter coat is thick already. Kinda muddy, though."

Such a tiny little person, yet she showed no fear at

all. I thought she might be settling in for a good long story about my breed, but the gate swung open and Mrs. Maiden came running into the pasture. Claire hopped up fast and tried to hide away behind me. "Uh-oh," she said.

"Claire!" Mrs. Maiden yelled. "Why did you run off? From now on, you only come out here with an adult — at least until you're older and more experienced. Do you understand?" Mrs. Maiden took a deep breath.

Claire looked at the ground. "I'm sorry, Mrs. Maiden. I'm sorry, Mother."

A grown-up who looked a lot like Claire stroked the girl's hair. "I asked you to wait with the older girls while I was in the office with Mrs. Maiden."

"But I saw the Belgian, just like in the book we read, remember? I wanted to meet him," Claire tried to explain.

The woman took Claire's hand and started toward the barn. I followed behind them.

"So, you know a lot about horses, Claire?" Mrs. Maiden asked. "Let's see how well you know your breeds. I said you'd be riding Daisy this morning, right? She's a gray Welsh cob. Find Daisy for me."

Claire nodded. She looked to the mare field where Gwen and her mares grazed just across the fence line. "There! There's a Welsh cob — a flea-bitten gray. And look beside her, a Hanoverian! She's so beautiful, a blood bay, and she has three socks."

Mrs. Maiden laughed at how smart Claire was about horses. "That's right! The Welsh is Daisy; Gwen is the Hanoverian. Now, let's see. Napoleon is a Shetland pony. Find Napoleon for me."

Claire giggled and pointed to Napoleon's rear end, sticking out from behind the hay ring. "That's easy!" she said. "There's the Shetland! He's a red roan."

"Really? You even know that?"

She was showing off then. "Yep! Red roan means a reddish coat that's sort of frosty white on top. Oh, but, Mrs. Maiden, I didn't know a Belgian lives here. Could I please ride him today?"

"No, not yet. He's a little big for you. Say good-bye to your friend, Macadoo. Let's go tack up Daisy. I'm sure you'll be riding Mac in no time."

I followed Claire to the gate and whinnied for her to return soon, which she did—with lots of treats! Mrs. Maiden was right. By winter, Claire joined me for a weekly vaulting lesson. By spring, she was proficient in most of the basic vaulting positions. Flank gave her more trouble than standing. By summer, she could even perform a special K—hands free of the surcingle at a trot. That summer, after Claire turned nine, she signed up for a week of riding camp. Mrs. Maiden let each child care for one horse during the entire week. Claire chose me.

"He's awfully big," warned Mrs. Maiden.

"I know!" Claire practically sang.

"During summer camp, you'll have to take care of Mac all by yourself. That means getting a mounting block so you can brush him and tack him up. And, at the end of the week, when we go camping up at the top of Saddle Mountain, you'll be in charge of Mac."

"Mrs. Maiden, I've been waiting all year just to take care of Mac during camp." Claire smelled my neck.

"What are you doing, Claire?"

"Nothing, giving Mac a good sniff." She smelled me again.

Mrs. Maiden kissed the top of Claire's head. "You are too cute. All right, Mac is yours. If he gets to be too much, let me know, and you can switch to Daisy."

Claire ran to the tack room for my brush box. "No way! It's Mac and me all the way! Thank you, Mrs. Maiden."

During camp we rode in the riding ring in the morning, went out on a trail ride across the Maury River and up Saddle Mountain after a short rest, and, sometimes, in the afternoon, played Chase Me Charlie in the ring.

Claire was not a fussy camper like some of the children who complained about dirt and sweat and hard work. She didn't mind picking rocks and gravel from my bare feet with her fingers. She would set the hoof pick down and explain, "I don't want to hurt your frog. That's a very sensitive part of your foot, I know." And, when it was too hot to ride, Claire was as happy to sit and read a book on my back as she was to get me all tacked up.

The highlight of riding camp for Maury River Stables campers was an overnight trip to the top of Saddle Mountain. The horses were packed with food and shelter for the campers and first-aid supplies for all of us. Stu loaded the truck with hay and grain and a barrel of water and drove our supplies up the logging trail, nearly to the crest of Saddle Mountain.

We reached the top with just enough daylight left for the children to pitch tents and for Stu to start a campfire. Long after nightfall, the campers were still swapping stories and songs. For the first time in my life I stood atop Saddle Mountain. The night sky glittered with stars, and I missed Izzy.

Claire loved the night sky just as my boy did. While the other campers and Mrs. Maiden slept inside their tents, Claire snuck outside with her sleeping bag, surrounded by the stars. Izzy would have done the same.

When Claire could not sleep, she grabbed my mane and hoisted herself up. She stretched out on my back, in much the same way Izzy had when I was still a colt. "See, up there's my favorite moon—and my dad's, too. A crescent moon." She sighed, as if waiting for something.

Claire pointed up. "There! Look! Mac, tonight is

the peak of the Perseids." The fire stars came fast and near, just as they had when I was a colt in Alberta. "My dad told me to stay awake tonight. Oh, Mac, Dad was right. I've never seen anything like this. Let's count them! I bet there's a million an hour, or at least a hundred. I call them shooting stars. My dad says they're meteors."

The stars seemed to descend, almost within reach. I hadn't made a wish in a very long time.

Claire knelt on my back, like in our vaulting lessons. She raised her hands high above her head, then stood up tall. When she could not reach the stars with her hands, she rose up on the very tips of her toes. She turned around and around, swaying her hands with the wind, dancing soft circles with her feet.

Between the two peaks of Saddle Mountain, I held Claire amid the Perseids. Quietly, she performed her freestyle routine. With no bridle, no surcingle, and no side reins, I stood square while Claire practiced leg passes with pointed toes, swung high up into scissors, and landed softly on my back. I imagined my back as broad and strong as the barn, and I imagined that like the great horse in the stars, I had wings, too. Wings to soar high enough to let Claire reach any dream.

The silence of Saddle Mountain settled into us. The Perseids, as Claire called the sky's display, began to fade. I dared wish nothing for myself.

CHAPTER THIRTY

Here for You, Always

For a year or more, it was as if Claire was my girl and I was her pony. True, when she competed, it was more often with Daisy, the Welsh, than with me. After the two returned to the barn from a hunter show — always with winning ribbons — haughty Daisy liked to trot over to the mare-gelding fence.

"*Whose* girl is Claire, again? Take a look at the blue ribbons on my stall door the next time you're allowed into the barn, Macadoo."

The bar across Daisy's stall door held so many ribbons that they often fell onto the floor and got trampled by girls and horses. "*I* won those ribbons for Claire," Daisy reminded me. "Not you."

Those ribbons were only the spoils of competition; they were not the spoils of the heart. When Claire wanted to catch the wind coming off the Maury River, she came to me. On the days that Claire felt like watching the clouds shift between the splendid mountains, she sat on my back in the field. And, most of all, Claire knew that one horse stood at the fence, always listening for Mrs. Maiden to call out, "Claire! Helmet!" To me, that was like "Tallyho!" was to the beagles and the hunters. I had only to hear "Claire! Helmet!" and look up from my hay, or grass, to see Claire sprinting toward my field. And Mrs. Maiden right behind her with a riding hat in hand.

"Mac, right here, my big boy." Claire clucked me over to her.

I was already there.

Claire would hop from the fence onto my back, grab mane, and we'd canter through the gelding field, around the run-in, down the line of cedar. She greeted every gelding we passed. The mares called to us from their field, and Claire would call back.

"Daisy! Princess! The fair Gwen!" She'd sing each of their names. She even knew the names of the boarders: "Secret! Lilac! Raven!" The mares raced beside us, though they did not outrace us. Claire liked to end our bareback adventures by galloping to the gate. Then, she'd slide to the ground and pat my neck. "What a good pony," Claire told me each time.

One day Claire arrived for her lesson and seemed a different girl from just a day earlier. Without a word, she groomed me. Without a pat to my shoulder, she tacked me up. She even forgot to offer me the carrot in her pocket.

In our riding lesson, Claire missed her diagonal. She got her hands all tangled up in the reins and fell out of her two-point and onto my neck.

Mrs. Maiden stopped the lesson. "Claire, what's going on this morning? We have a show to get ready for, and you're not paying attention. You're taking Mac like you wanted this time, but you're letting Mac carry the full load of the work for you today."

Claire steered me to the middle of the ring, where Mrs. Maiden stood. I felt the child shrug. "My st-stomach hurts," she complained.

"Are you sick?" Mrs. Maiden asked.

She started to cry and shook her head. "My mom and dad are getting a divorce. My d-d-dad moved out of our house. I don't want to show. I just want everything to be the same."

Mrs. Maiden touched Claire's leg. "Oh, sweetheart. It really hurts bad, doesn't it?"

"So bad," Claire said, and wrapped her arms

around my neck. She pressed her face to my mane and I could feel her tears through her fluttering eyelashes. A butterfly's kiss. I whickered and even more tears came, and she stopped trying to stop them.

Mrs. Maiden tried consoling her. "Listen to me, Claire. What your family is going through is hard. I understand if you don't want to show right now. Just remember that Mac is always here for you, darling, and so am I."

Claire skipped her next lesson and her next. I waited at the fence line, hoping for her return. Canada geese honked overhead in the fall. Some of them dropped out of formation, landed in our field, and lingered all the mild winter. In the spring, yellow warblers and indigo buntings arrived for nesting. Cabbage butterflies spiraled through our field in search of dandelion nectar. Stu repaired fences and jumps. New cars brought new students to the Maury River Stables. I listened for Claire or the sound of Mrs. Maiden reminding her, "Claire, helmet!"

How could I always be there for someone who might never return?

With the warmer weather, I missed Claire sitting on me in the field when she felt lazy, or walking with me by the river when she went looking for phoebes and king-fishers. I wanted to canter around the pasture with her and race the mares again.

All during Claire's absence, Eric Sand still attended his weekly lessons, and he needed me not to miss Claire when I was with him.

Maybe, I thought, *I can always be there for Claire by always being there for Eric.*

I made sure to greet Eric every time with a soft whicker.

"Mac," he would say. "We're best friends now."

He had grown in strength and improved in horsemanship. He held the reins himself and rode tall, and alone, in the saddle. When Eric said, "Whoa," and pulled back on my reins, I stopped and waited. He learned to hold the reins lightly, and, though he could not squeeze his legs with great control, his seat and his trunk instructed me when to go. So I did as he asked; I walked on. All the while, Claire stayed away from the Maury River Stables.

When the horse center in Lexington hosted a dazzling moonlight show to raise money for therapeutic riding, Eric Sand showed me.

Mrs. Maiden insisted that every pair representing the Maury River Stables be impeccably turned out. She braided my mane and tail, so that I would impress the judges. I had grown to love Mrs. Maiden and cherished those rare moments when it was just the two of us.

"What would I do without you, Macadoo? Every

child at the barn loves you! Just look at how you've helped Eric. And not just in the saddle; he's developed more strength and control than anyone thought he could. And he is forever smiling, too! Why do you think that is?" she asked me.

I whickered for Mrs. Maiden to tell me the answer.

"Because of you, that's why. Because that little boy loves this Belgian. And I do, too." She kissed my cheek and finished the last of the braiding. "Now you're ready! I predict we'll be coming home with a slew of ribbons."

At the horse center, Eric wore the crisp blue jacket of a hunter and a black velvet hat, just as Claire wore when showing with Daisy. Everyone called us a handsome team.

In our classes, Virgil Sand and his wife walked beside me. Eric listened to the judge, as did I. I waited for Eric, though, to ask me to walk, to halt, to reverse, to back up, and to trot. At the end of our first class, we lined up in a row and waited for the judge's decision. Eric waved to Mrs. Maiden; she gave us a thumbs-up. When I heard the announcer say, "First place goes to Eric Sand on Macadoo, owned by the Maury River Stables," I bowed my head.

Eric Sand won two blue ribbons, one red, and one white; he won them with me. He took the ribbons back to the barn and placed them on my door. Virgil Sand brought me a basket of apples.

After some boarders in the barn—Cowboy and Charlie—moved out, Mrs. Maiden moved Gwen and me into stalls next to each other. It was hard for us to really visit when we were always turned out in separate fields, so I was glad to have her near me.

When Claire first left and I felt the strain of tangles starting again, I reached out to Gwen for help. "Is this what Mamere meant? Will I always long for someone I love to come back to me? Is missing someone the Belgian way?" I asked my friend.

"I suppose that is our way—all of us—not just Belgian horses, but any horse who must both let go of and hold on to a person."

"Why does it hurt so much when someone you love goes away?"

As Mamere and Job often did, Gwen shared her grain with me. "Oh, Macadoo, remember love comes back in ways and at times you least expect. Do you believe this?"

I ate the grain. I inhaled it and wished I had left some for later. Grateful that the top part of our wall, made of bars, allowed us to see and nuzzle each other, I blew onto Gwen. "I would like to believe it, but how?"

"Look around you." She offered the last of her grain. "Look around. We are home, and we are loved. Every day we are loved."

Neither of us wore blankets that night. Spring

had come early, yet the night was so warm it seemed that even spring was keen to move on. I stood guard at my window, wondering if learning to love my work might mean never again giving a child my whole heart. Whenever I did love a child, that child moved on, and then my heart ached.

Will every child I love go away? I wondered. *If I offer my service but not my heart to my students,* I thought, *maybe the separation I know is coming won't hurt so bad.*

Then I realized that to build such a wall was not at all the Belgian way. My heart belonged already to Eric Sand, too, and also still to Poppa and Izzy, Naomi, and Claire, and already to those new friends I had yet to meet.

CHAPTER THIRTY-ONE

The Old App

Early one day in March, nearly a year after Claire had gone away, Mrs. Maiden came with breakfast and with news. I heard Stu hammering fence posts and car wheels crunching on the gravel drive.

Mrs. Maiden stepped into my stall, gave me my grain, and tossed in three flakes of hay, and I nickered for a fourth. I finished before anyone else, and, eager to be in the sunshine, I stuck my head out the window to smell the apple buds. Mrs. Maiden interrupted my daydream of eating all the young buds on Saddle Mountain.

"Hello, Mac. Guess what! Claire's come back."

I looked around to find the girl.

Mrs. Maiden set down my brush box, took out the comb, and started pulling the briars out of my forelock and mane. "Claire's not the same little person we knew last year. I know she'll be glad to see you. Let her know you remember her. Remind her that her old friends at the Maury River Stables still care for her," she said.

But it was Ann, a new girl whom I had just met, not Claire, that led me into the riding ring for a lesson, taught by Stu. Claire stayed close by Mrs. Maiden and didn't join the other students. Mrs. Maiden was busy welcoming a new horse.

"He's beautiful," I heard Claire say, though the horse was anything but. The gelding was dim and drained of life. Sunken and hollow. Covered with cuts and scrapes. His hooves overgrown and splintered.

He struggled to lift his head. Dehydration, I thought, had set in. His bones stuck out. He had hollows and crooks where I had muscle and mass. He bled from deep cuts that made his legs shaky, but Claire saw something more.

In a small voice that also sounded drained and dimmed, Claire now stuttered. "Ch-Chancey's b-beautiful." She kissed the new old horse on his cheek. He nuzzled her and nickered.

And then I saw something in him, too. His heart.

Despite all the old App had been through, he was rallying to receive and return the love of the child who stood before him.

The paper birch quivered in the spring breeze and drew from me a buried memory of a season past at Cedarmont, when a boy reached out for my cheek in much the same way.

"Everything will be okay." I heard Claire try to reassure Chancey like Izzy had done for me.

The other students didn't see Chancey in the same way.

"Ewww, he's ugly. What's wrong with him?" I heard Ann say.

Mrs. Maiden defended him. "Give Chancey some time. His owner lost her land, her barn, and all of her horses. For the last six months, Chancey's been left out in a pasture with no one to feed or water or care for him. Had to fight his way through barbed wire for fresh water. He's a tough old Appy; he'll be fine, especially if we give him lots of love and care."

"If he's an Appaloosa, where are his spots?"

Stu laughed. "He's got no spots! He's what you call cremello. Like a partial albino. That's why Isbell — Mrs. Maiden — put the fly mask on him. See how his skin is pink?"

Mrs. Maiden turned Chancey out into our paddock. The other geldings, led by Dante, crowded around the gate to watch. The Appy squealed when she turned him loose, and he tried to run. Dante pushed him into the fence; Chancey squealed again and slipped in the soft mud—another signal of spring's arrival—that had formed around the gate.

Claire ran into our field, flinging her arms at Dante. "Leave him alone, Dante!" She chased the Thoroughbred away. Chancey followed Claire back to the gate, and long after she had left, he stood up to his fetlocks in standing water and mud, waiting until after dark for her return. When he realized she wouldn't return until daylight, he grazed alone and kept to himself, well out of the way.

Where am I needed most? How can I best serve Claire, Mrs. Maiden, and the Maury River Stables today? I asked myself. And the answer came to me: *Chancey.*

From down at the water tub, I heard a squeal. Dante had Chancey's fly mask in his teeth. He cantered and bucked and tossed it to the ground. Napoleon picked it up. Chancey did not give chase, for Chancey could hardly see. Years of standing unprotected in the sun had damaged his fair eyes.

I raced down the hill to defend him. "Go away," I told Chancey when I reached him. "Follow your nose to the hay ring!"

It had been a long, long time since I had raced. I cantered straight for Dante. "I am Macadoo, Draft

King of the Maury River! Try to beat me if you dare!" I cried out.

As I reached Dante, I galloped the last few strides to bolster the sound of my two thousand pounds. I stopped short in the Thoroughbred's face.

"I want his fly mask." I pinned my ears and flared out my nostrils. "Go and get it from the Shetland," I demanded.

Dante snorted and turned his back to me.

I knew he could trace his hot-blooded lineage back hundreds of years to the stallions of the Orient. All Thoroughbreds can. Dante had won a fortune on the track and then lost his way. He had something to prove to everyone he met, but he still hadn't proven himself a dependable school horse. Only the most advanced students at the Maury River Stables dared to mount him. Few of them, even, stayed with him for long. Mrs. Maiden had not given up on him, but Dante didn't make it easy on her. I would not make it easy for him, I decided.

The Thoroughbred pressed his mouth into my maimed ear, but I did not quiver.

"No man could break me on the ground, though many tried. I was broke in the Maury River because only the water could quell my fire." He pawed the ground and boasted, "I am King of the Maury River! Not you."

Then and there, I challenged Dante for the herd. And that gave Chancey time to eat hay from the far corner. Free and unbothered, for once, he ate.

I drew a mark on the ground and dared Dante to cross. That gave the Appy even more time. "You can keep your stories of being broken by the river," I said to Dante. "As a yearling, I overtook my own father, a Belgian stallion descended from the Great Horse of Flanders!"

I preened my chest and shook out my mane. I outweighed the black gelding by far and could easily have beat any horse in the pasture. Only the butterflies of our field knew for certain that I would never fight. Dante backed down.

"Napoleon," I called. "Bring the fly mask to me."

The Shetland carried Chancey's mask between his teeth, and he dropped it at my feet. Just for good measure, I let loose a bodacious sneeze, spraying Dante with timothy and clover. And, with that, the fight was over.

From then on, the geldings left Chancey alone. Though the old App made no other friends in the field, and none of the other barn girls or their mothers paid him any attention either, he had friends in Claire and Gwen and me.

Claire, Gwen, and I all helped the old App. In the ring or the paddock or the barn, at least one of us was always there. Mrs. Maiden helped us grow closer by keeping our stalls side by side. This way, I could share my grain with Chancey whenever he needed something extra.

What restored Chancey also restored Claire. She returned to her riding lessons and to the show ring. As Chancey adjusted to his new home and came to trust Claire, his confidence returned and so did Claire's. But our work would soon be sorely tested.

CHAPTER THIRTY-TWO

The Watch

One night, when Chancey returned from showing at Tamworth Springs without Claire, Gwen came out of the mares' shelter and called me to the fence. "Macadoo, watch over our friend tonight. Claire fell today at the show when the old App ducked out of a jump. Claire's been hurt. Her father condemned Chancey."

"Chancey would never hurt Claire. What happened?" I asked.

"He couldn't see the jump on the approach. Daisy rode home with him and says he's in a bad way. Chancey may be colicking. Go help him."

A storm moved across Saddle Mountain and enveloped our field with a brutal wind and heavy rain. I knew Chancey's place, at the cedar, and found him there, rolling in the grips of colic. He pawed at his belly and bit at the tangles clenching him inside.

"Come on, Chancey. Get up." I pushed him up and we paced the ridgetop. In the face of his greatest fear, I did not leave him alone, but kept him moving. "Walk on. You must walk." I blew across his face. "What is it, friend? Why are you afraid?"

"I am old, Macadoo. I am old and am going blind. This place is my last chance."

Chancey was right. He likely would not survive the auction house. Old and ill horses fare poorly at such places. Like the Thoroughbred filly, I know Chancey was worth something more. He had already won a child's heart, and he had joined up with mine.

"Haven't you noticed?" And then I told him just what Gwen had told me. "We live among friends now. We are loved."

CHAPTER THIRTY-THREE

A Gentle Peace

One afternoon, Chancey and I waited at the gate for our students to arrive, as we did every day. I heard the familiar knocking of a truck engine. Our vet, Doctor Russ, whom I had known most of my life, was making his barn call for vaccinations, like he did twice yearly. In the distance I saw him pull into the drive. Before I could tell Chancey, he told me, "Doctor Russ is here."

"Old App, you'd know that sound from the other side of Saddle Mountain. Yes, the vet is here. Today is needle day again," I rumbled.

We walked toward the barn; Chancey moved slowly, following my scent and the sound of my feet.

The second I halted, Chancey asked, "Why have we stopped? Is something the matter?" He couldn't see anything but he sensed that I saw something startling.

"No, it's . . . someone's with Doctor Russ. Someone—"

The mares whinnied as Doctor Russ and his guest passed by their field. A heap of curly red hair—someone that I remembered losing such a long time ago— caused my front legs to buckle. My knees skimmed the grass, my heart caught fire, and I whickered to an old friend, my first friend.

"Who do you see?" Chancey wanted to know.

"Izzy," I told my dear Appy. "I see my boy Izzy."

True, he was no longer a boy. He was now a young man, and with the same curious eyes, walking toward us with a notebook in his hand. Could I have stopped myself from whinnying over and over?

No, and I didn't try. For a long time, I had imagined this reunion every day. My Izzy, lost like the star Mira, was back.

With great joy, I galloped to him.

"Macadoo! It's me!" Izzy called me to him. He held his arms open, my halter resting on his shoulder—still the same one that John Macadoo gave me when I was a new colt to this valley, though now it just barely fits on the last buckle. I nickered and nuzzled him as if he were still a boy.

"I've brought my new assistant with me today, Macadoo. You know this young man, I believe," said Doctor Russ.

"Macadoo, you're still right here at Saddle Mountain. You waited for me, boy, all these years."

Izzy held my halter out to me and I lowered my head for him. We walked to the barn together, and while Doctor Russ vaccinated me for influenza and strangles, rabies and West Nile and a host of other threats, Izzy stood by me.

"I can't believe it's you! My first horse, Mac. You were right, Doctor Russ. Mac seems to remember me."

Doctor Russ looked up from his work. "Oh, he remembers you, all right. He came cantering over as soon as he saw you. I expect he's just as glad that you didn't forget him."

"Forget Mac? Never. Mac is the one who helped Poppa and me become a family after Mom died." Izzy scratched my poll. "Never met a better horse. Who could ever forget Mac?"

Mrs. Maiden overheard him and came over to my stall. "You know, I was about ready to give up the barn when I bought Mac, Izzy."

"Really? What made you take him, then?" Izzy asked.

She shook her head. "I guess I thought maybe if he was just the right horse, a gentle, willing, reliable school horse, then I could add more lessons, and we could revive the vaulting team and expand the therapeutic program. The Maury River Stables has really grown since Mac came here. Tell Judge Isler I said thank you."

Izzy smiled and patted my withers. "I will, Mrs. Maiden. I was so sad when Mac left. Even now, when I look at the stars, I think of Mac. Would you ever sell him back to me?"

Mrs. Maiden laughed. "I know it was hard on you to let him go. No. No, I could never sell this horse. He has helped so many children; you can't imagine. Mac is every child's favorite horse, and it seems like every student is his favorite child."

Outside the barn, Stu greeted Eric Sand. It was time for our lesson, and Eric needed me. I nuzzled Izzy's neck and hoped he would come back with Doctor Russ again. I whickered to Mrs. Maiden and tugged on my lead rope toward where I could hear Stu and Eric talking.

"Mac knows Eric is here. Why don't you stay and watch him work, Izzy?"

"I wish I could, but Doctor Russ and I still have three more calls to make," he said.

"You know, Mac will always be here when you want to visit him," she said.

Mrs. Maiden was right. Like Izzy taught me, friendship is like Mira Stella, the star that shines even when it cannot be seen. And Mamere was right, too, when she said, "Even when you can no longer see me, I am here."

Good friends have come and gone from my life, and each one remains in my heart. I love Izzy, and I love them all.

I know I am blessed to have lived with Mamere for a time. She placed a vision on my heart, not of the horse I was, but of the horse I could become. Without her vision, I would have given up.

Could any colt have asked for a more patient friend than Job? Or one smarter than Molly? At the Virginia auction, the Thoroughbred filly reminded me how to take one step toward my purpose. And when I had given up on finding even one forever friendship, I met Gwen, then Chancey. I am here for them.

I am here for Janey and John Macadoo and Poppa, too. For Doctor Russ. For my Izzy. For Eric Sand, Naomi, and Claire. And, for Isbell Maiden. For all my students.

Some girls and boys come to ride; others just want to sit and comb the briars from my mane with their small fingers. Children tell me stories of home, stories of play and work. I know that children have problems that can more easily be solved with a friend to lighten the load. I am here for each of them.

I have learned that with or without my dam, with or without my boy, if I can step out into a field surrounded by mountains, under the care of the same great shining star that has always nourished me, in service of a child or an equine or a kind man or woman, I will find the heart to walk on.

My father predicted that I would never forget him, and it's true. I will always remember. All my life I have carried his burden with me, the heaviest load of all.

And until I take my last breath, every night under the stars I make a lasting wish on my father's behalf: *Humans and horses have done such good together—built cities, kingdoms, and nations—but our most important building is yet undone. The world needs us now more than ever to bring a gentle peace. Working together, side by side, as we have for centuries. So, do not let us horses be forgotten. Any of us. We are here for you, always.*

Author's Note

My daughter was five years old the first time I saw the power of horses to make a child smile, laugh, and believe anything is possible. On the day of her first riding lesson, I watched her lift a pony's foot to pick out rocks that had gotten stuck in its hooves, saw her concentrate so hard to steer that pretty pony around the ring, and heard her giggle with delight at her pony's breath on her neck after the lesson.

My little girl is twenty now. Back then, I was working many hours a week at a new job. As a family, we were dealing with upheaval and uncertainty brought about by divorce. The barn became a respite for us both — a place far away from the "real world," where nothing much mattered except for the horses and their power to make you forget or make you remember — whichever you needed most.

I was thirty-three when I started riding with my girl, thirty-six when we bought our first horse, and forty-two the first (and only) time I competed. Together, my daughter and I have ridden mules in national forests, jumped horses over logs and fences and narrow creeks, and played polo on ponies in a dusty field. We've cantered through pastureland and mountain trails and have been led by sure-footed equines safely down steep, rocky cliffs. As my daughter grew up, we were connected through our love of horses, a gift my daughter gave to me.

For thousands of years, people have shared the earth with horses. They've been our partners in tilling soil and winning wars, clearing land and transporting us to places both near and far. The power that horses have brought to my life has not so much to do with the power of physical strength or endurance or hard work, though these are surely good lessons I've learned from my *Equus ferus caballus* friends. I'm thinking more of the power of spirit—the power that comes from being present to the day, of remembering to breathe, and of discovering a shared language not of words but of feelings, images, and tiny gestures.

I am forty-eight years old and only just now beginning to understand that for all these years, horses have not been taking me away from the "real world" but bringing me there. After all, what could be more real than being still and silent outdoors with a friend, listening to birds of the meadow and forest settle down, watching the moon rise, and knowing you are loved?

Acknowledgments

Thank you to my early readers: Judith Amateau, Leigh Amateau, the Gryder family, Julie McConnell, Maggie Menard, and Elena Zerkin.

I thank my beautiful friend Meg Medina, who encouraged me to keep trying to get Mac's story right when I got off course (for a few years).

Much love and gratitude to these horses and mules who inspired me: Jake, Beau, Kurt, My Sweet Albert, Norman, Mia, Firecracker, July Johnson, Ike, Opie, Latte, and Dart. And these good people: Maddy, Little Alex, Kathy, Deb Sensabaugh, Cheryl Pallant, Patty Summers, and Jennifer Wright, DVM. And thanks also to the James River Writers community.

Thank you, Vicki and the vaulting team in Maidens, Virginia. I will never forget your beauty and grace on that amber Indian summer night with the sun setting, the moon rising, and Kurt holding you aloft. Thank you all so much for sharing your enthusiasm for vaulting and your love of horses with me. Rest in peace, Kurt, your sweet and steady teammate.

Thank you to my fine Writers House team: Leigh Feldman and her assistant, Jean Garnett.

Always, always, always, I'm so grateful for the Candlewick magic. Thank you, Sherry Fatla, Rachel Smith, Maryellen Hanley, Nicole Raymond, Kate Herrmann, Martha Dwyer, Betsy Uhrig, Erika Denn, and Tracy Miracle. Thank you, especially, to my extraordinary editors, Karen Lotz and Kate Fletcher.

I am blessed to belong to a generous, loving family and would mostly like to thank my daughter and friend, Judith, and my partner into infinity and beyond, Bubba.

Questions to Consider

1. Macadoo is the narrator of his own story. How is a horse's perspective on the world different from a human's? If Macadoo could visit your neighborhood, what would catch his eye?

2. After his first and only meeting with his father, Macadoo ends up with a badly chewed-up ear. Why does the stallion maim his son?

3. "If you don't find your purpose, son," says Macadoo's father, "you'll end up like me" (page 9). How did Macadoo's father lose his way? Why does he believe that his life has no purpose? Is he right or wrong? Why?

4. Machines now do most of the jobs that Belgian horses once did. What sort of work is still being done by animals? What jobs that are currently performed by humans can you imagine machines doing in the future?

5. Izzy and Macadoo were separated from their mothers at an early age, and both are growing up without fathers. How does each cope with his loss? How do they help each other recover?

6. "I've lived my entire life in fear of tomorrow," Macadoo's mother tells him (page 42). Why was she always afraid of the future? After she and Macadoo separate, what do you imagine happens to her?

7. "Equines need to belong," Macadoo realizes (page 45). "We are whole when we are part of the whole." Is the same also true for humans? Do you need to be around others in order to feel fully yourself? Do some people make you feel more like yourself?

8. Macadoo understands human speech, but he can't speak it himself. How does he communicate with people?

9. "Helping others is what makes you great," Macadoo's mother tells her son when he is a yearling (page 15). "That's your purpose." How does he keep proving her right?

10. Why does Izzy show Mira Stella, the wonderful star, to Macadoo? What makes the star distinctive? How does it bring hope and comfort to Macadoo?

11. "Mrs. Maiden says you change people's lives in the therapeutic school," Macadoo says to his friend Gwen (page 144). How does Macadoo himself change Eric's life? How does he change Claire's? How do they change his?

12. What role does the Virginia countryside play in this novel? How does it affect Macadoo? How does it help others heal?

13. Macadoo has his mother's gentleness, but he is also his father's son. When does he demonstrate the fighting side of his breeding? Why? How does the incident also illustrate what makes him so different from his father?

14. Belgian horses like Macadoo need a purpose, and so do humans. When Izzy grows up, what is his purpose? What would you like your purpose to be when you're an adult?

15. The book ends with the wish that Macadoo makes every night. Do you think it will come true? Why or why not?

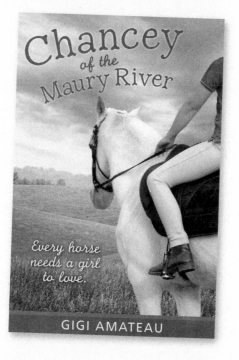

Everyone had great expectations for Dante's Inferno, grandson of the greatest racehorse of modern times. But when Dante doesn't live up to his bloodlines, can he find redemption as an eventing horse?

Available in hardcover and audio and as an e-book.

Read on for an excerpt . . .

CHAPTER ONE

JUST BREATHE

Come on. Breathe."

Those are the first words I heard in my life. I had been foaled just ahead of spring, in a deep freeze of winter. Arrived on a night when the world outside was encased in ice and the world inside was draped in dark.

Most Thoroughbreds are born in April or May, after the snow has melted and the ground has thawed. But the truth is, birthdays don't mean all that much to most horses.

Oh, getting here early by a few months can give a racing colt or filly a boost during that first year. Early foals, like me, will likely be bigger, stronger, and faster than the later babies. After that, the actual date of birth matters not a hill of beans nor a field of hay. Nobody

an excerpt from *Dante of the Maury River*

remembers, after a while, whether you were born in winter or spring or any other season, because once the New Year rolls in, we Thoroughbreds reset our birthdays to the first day of January.

For the record, I came into the world during February. February fourteenth to be exact. Way early for foaling season, but there's always an early one.

I can still recall the pause between my first breath and the next. Quite a disruption, for sure. An entire universe of wonder and beauty between breathing in and breathing out. A full-on leave-it-all-on-the-dirt meeting between inspiration and expiration.

"Breathe, breathe," the man yelled at the moment of my entry into this world. To be honest, I didn't understand a lick of what he was saying or have any inkling what he meant for me to do.

I could feel his tired skin pressing against mine, and I felt his heavy breath hovering over me.

"Let's get his heart going," he said, but I couldn't figure out to who-all he might be speaking. Everything was dark.

He kneaded my chest, then he jibbed and jabbed at my heart, and that hurt.

Up till then, I had only ever known the warmth and protection of my dam, but now I felt an icy wind through the shed's thin walls and it chilled me to the bone.

an excerpt from *Dante of the Maury River*

I couldn't figure out what was happening, but I got this much: something was going wrong.

"Come on," the man begged again. He crouched low and massaged my chest with his palm. Pounded on me hard. That hurt, too, but I was helpless.

The man spoke directly to me. "Twenty-five years ago I attended a delivery on a night exactly like this one. A colt. Your grandfather, Dante's Paradiso."

Marey stirred in the corner, but I was far from her in body and moving on in spirit. She whickered. "Please. Your family needs you. Don't give up. Breathe. Give me one breath."

"Breathe" made sense when Marey said it.

I took exactly one, just like Marey asked me to do. Then instead of grabbing for another, I turned around back from where I had come, searching for that sweet, lush limbo where nobody had to tell me what to do because there everything was open and natural and free. And there, I was part of everything.

Though I had a powerful yearning to stay with Marey, I had an even stronger one to leave my body behind. Even before life was fully mine, I longed to go somewhere else.

"Try," Marey whispered toward me, motionless.

I drifted away not because I didn't love her but because I felt a stronger pull beckoning.

an excerpt from *Dante of the Maury River*

"You are destined to follow your grandfather. Please, just try, son. Please."

She nickered softly.

Then, I expired. Let it all go.

I bounced between light and dark, cold and heat. A golden net lit up the barn and wrapped me in its folds. My spirit hovered above the foaling floor, watching the effort to revive my body below. Steam curled up from that new little black colt lying on the cold ground. Groping hands reached out to rub life into me. The man bent over my chest, but not even his sharp breath could pierce the cold pall around my heart.

an excerpt from *Dante of the Maury River*

CHAPTER TWO

BLOODLINES

The distant sound of hoofbeats lured me from the cold foaling shed. Along a broad, starlit pathway that stretched out at my feet, Thoroughbreds from my bloodlines across the ages surrounded me. Upon my word and honor, I testify that I knew each one by scent and sound even though we had never met. These ancestors warmed me with their own breaths and led me through land and water and sky.

Honest to thunder, I didn't even consider staying in that hard frozen place. I stood happily among my pedigree, amid a brilliant rolling landscape far beyond the foaling barn back in Kentucky.

Now, some might say I'm getting a tad carried away in my imagination, but consider this: we all possess

an excerpt from *Dante of the Maury River*

ancestral memory. Every one of us knows and remembers places, faces, words, and triumphs of spirit and flesh that we have not lived but that, somehow, we know to be true. Knowledge and memory come to us through our bloodlines. And that's a fact.

I had left my dam and my body behind, refused to take that second breath, and, in doing so, transitioned from a dim place to a brilliant one. While the vet worked to revive my body, and while my dam rested in the corner nickering quiet encouragement, I walked alongside my dam's father, my grandfather, the first Dante. Dante's Paradiso.

"Why am I here?" I asked the stallion.

"You've arrived now because the pedigree needs you," Grandfather Dante replied. "The breed needs you. This is the time for a new kind of champion, but you must conquer three great tests. We're all counting on you."

"What if I fail?"

Grandfather Dante snapped his tail against my barrel. Then he touched his nose to mine, and my heart twitched. The smell of damp grass on his muzzle made me remember Marey.

The horizon in his world was swathed in emerald and violet-gray grass. Grandfather Dante and I, both as black as night, stood together under the golden stars. "I don't want to go back," I confessed.

an excerpt from *Dante of the Maury River*